About the Author

Robert Welbourn was born and bred in Yorkshire and has lived there almost all his life. He's had a passion for books for as long as he can remember and has been writing his whole life. His favourite authors are Bret Easton Ellis and Stephen King, and he cites Ellis as his number-one influence. Outside of books he has a passion for travel and cats. And his friends and family, etc.

He studied English Literature at Salford University and this confirmed that he wanted to spend his life working with books, one way or another.

IDEAL ANGELS

IDEAL ANGELS

ROBERT WELBOURN

Unbound

London

This edition first published in 2018

Unbound

6th Floor Mutual House, 70 Conduit Street, London W1S 2GF

www.unbound.com

ISBN (eBook): 9781911586791

ISBN (Paperback): 9781911586784

Design by Mecob

Cover image:
© Shutterstock.com

Printed in Great Britain by Clays Ltd, Elcograf S.p.A

Dear Reader,

The book you are holding came about in a rather different way to most others. It was funded directly by readers through a new website: Unbound.

Unbound is the creation of three writers. We started the company because we believed there had to be a better deal for both writers and readers. On the Unbound website, authors share the ideas for the books they want to write directly with readers. If enough of you support the book by pledging for it in advance, we produce a beautifully bound special subscribers' edition and distribute a regular edition and e-book wherever books are sold, in shops and online.

This new way of publishing is actually a very old idea (Samuel Johnson funded his dictionary this way). We're just using the internet to build each writer a network of patrons. Here, at the back of this book, you'll find the names of all the people who made it happen.

Publishing in this way means readers are no longer just passive consumers of the books they buy, and authors are free to write the books they really want. They get a much fairer return too – half the profits their books generate, rather than a tiny percentage of the cover price.

If you're not yet a subscriber, we hope that you'll want to join our publishing revolution and have your name listed in one of our books in the future. To get you started, here is a £5 discount on your first pledge. Just visit unbound.com, make your pledge and type ELOISE18 in the promo code box when you check out.

Thank you for your support,

Dan, Justin and John
Founders, Unbound

Super Patrons

Paul Amourdedieu
Ian Anderson
Tim Atkinson
Karen Attwood
Alex Barnett
Gareth Butler
Mary Caldwell
Ally Caldwell
Richard Clayton
Tamsen Courtenay
Neal Cowan
RA Enzor
Niall Flack
Sophie Goodman
Christine Goodson
Elliot & Naomi Harper
Naomi Harper
Mike Hodgson
Tony Hua
Mickey Insley
Ed Ireland
Gerald Jennings
Hannah Jennings
Dan Kieran
Sandy Marshall
Callum Mitchell
John Mitchinson
Paul Murphy
Rod Murray
Jamie Oliver
Gregory Olver
Michael Paley

Stephen Phelps
Lyndon Phillips
Justin Pollard
Simon Riordan
Chris Ryall
James Smith
Anthony Squelch
Neil Taylor
Peter Welbourn
Jonathan & Sophie Welbourn
Andrew Welbourn
David Wheatley
Alex Williams
Steve Wisdom

With grateful thanks to David Wheatley who helped to make this book happen.

0

Tumescent, tumescence, a rush of blood but not to the head. The anger gives way to resignation, betrayal turns into hopelessness. Despair is everywhere.

Your world is different from mine. Your forever stretches from first matter to last. Mine is the blink of an eye. There was darkness before, and that darkness will come again. You can't control it, you can't swim. There is only sinking. You can try to hedge your bets, you can plan for what is coming, but you cannot stop it coming. From the top of the highest height, you feel like you can see everything, but you cannot. You are blind. But the blindness is not the darkness, because the darkness is not black. It is so much more. It is like your eyes are inside out, and everything you see is inverted in a way your brain cannot comprehend. It threatens to tear you apart. You know you will eventually be torn apart, but you do not know how. Not yet. You will not know until it happens, and by then it will already be too late. It will not be a she, or a him, but it will be a you. You will tear yourself apart searching for a meaning that does not exist. You will kick and scream and scratch and cry and bleed and it will all be for naught. It has already been done. Everything that ever is, ever has been, or ever will be is already done. You cannot stop it. You cannot control it. You can only accept it. You know you will not be able to, but you can try. You can pretend. You can fake. You are a fake. Your whole life has been a fake. Everything is nothing. But this is OK. This is not necessarily a bad thing. You are...

You are...

In that darkness there is a light, and in this light there is a promise. The promise is her name, the promise is that maybe everything will be OK. But you know it can never be, the promise is a lie, so you stop thinking, you stop feeling, the light goes out and you continue.

1

I am so sorry, but I must leave you now. I have tried and I have tried, but I have failed. She cannot join me, and so I must join her. Do not mourn for me – I died a long time ago. Know that I love you and I do not do this to hurt you. I'll watch over you, I'll always be with you.

2

It starts on a Friday night. You get up from your desk after a particularly unproductive day and your plan is to go home, pick up some food for the weekend and eat too much, specifically not drink, work out. But someone you work with invites you to the pub and your lack of self-restraint is evident as you immediately say yes. And you go to the pub, sip that first beer and think maybe next weekend, next month, next year, maybe in another lifetime, maybe when you give a shit. And you sip the beer and remember why you have no self-restraint – it isn't just the taste, it's the promise of being drunk, of the freedom that being drunk brings, of not caring anymore, and that's when you meet her.

You notice her immediately, she's too beautiful for you not to. You don't recognise her. Then again you don't recognise a lot of the people who may or may not be there with the people you may or may not be there with. You haven't worked for the company long, it's a fairly large company, the building you work in is five floors, you rarely leave your desk except to get a drink or to take a piss, spending your days sitting staring at your computer, staring into oblivion, so there's every chance she does work with you. In any case you ignore her, not specifically shutting her out, but rather not talking to her through lack of knowing how to initiate yourself into other people's lives. You talk to the people you know, the people from your team, the other two teams adjacent to yours, people you have spoken to before, safe people.

You sit at a table, sipping beer, watching people drift away. One woman has to go home to her husband – tea will be ready soon so she can't be late. One man has a gig the following day, an all-dayer in a different city, so he also can't be out too late. This isn't rock and roll, this is adult life. You tried to live the rock and roll lifestyle once upon a time, but not anymore. Being a not-especially-well-off adult with rent and bills doesn't allow for much rock-and-roll excitement. Regardless, it is Friday night, you've worked hard (well, worked anyway) all week and now is your time to relax. A weekend of not drinking turns into a shot of sambuca, and this is when you know it's over. Saturday is not going to be fun. But Saturday is tomorrow, today is Friday and Friday is now, the future can worry about itself, the consequences will happen to another you, a future you. This is the present you, and the present you wants to drink.

Before you know it there are just four of you remaining; people have drifted off into their lives, into their obligations, but not you. You have no obligations. You, two men you work with and the girl. The way these two talk to her you think she must work with you, why else would she be here, you hope she does so you might see her in the office, but if she doesn't so what? The four of you are at a table and you find yourself sitting next to her, and another of the great qualities of being drunk swells up inside you, and you find yourself talking to her. At first you're not listening, your main concern being trying not to stare. You have to look at her, so as not to seem ignorant, but you don't want to leer. You're prone to leering at the best of times, let alone under the influence of alcohol, or whatever else may come your way, and so for a long time you don't know what she's saying. She's too beautiful to be understood, her words must be on another level, another plane, you don't occupy the same time and space as them, as her. Long, centre-parted black hair – not naturally black but it suits her, complements her pale skin. Her eyes are green, amazing – you can see enough behind them and inside them to think maybe this one is something else, maybe this one is like you, maybe this one is not like them. Her nose, slightly large, protrudes from her face, but not in a bad way, it does not ruin anything that's in front of you. It's the kind of slight imperfection that can make you love someone even more. Love? You must be drunk.

She smiles often, warmly, perfect white teeth emerging from behind perfect red lips, a smile you keep trying to coax out of her, and which you seem to be able to do with almost alarming regularity. She wears a white tank top, black bra (you can't help but notice, she's not exactly trying to hide it), blue jeans; she's skinny but not so much so that it's off-putting, not the kind of model thin that makes you worry you might break her – she's just the size you like. This sounds creepier than you mean it to, but you know (or at least hope) the words are only in your head; no one around the table says anything so they must be, thank God, or whatever it is you believe in right now – life, love, sex, breasts, alcohol. You can see the shape of her breasts, you can imagine what they look like and how they feel, the thought making you equal parts horny and aching – horny in your groin, aching in your heart. You can see the shape of her hips through her jeans, and you imagine them too. You imagine lifting her up by the hips, holding her in your arms and you take another drink and dismiss the thought. It's not healthy. Not yet anyway.

Eventually you're able to listen, and completely engage in the conversation, alcohol permitting anyway. You find out she's a big reader like yourself, another plus. You ask what she's currently reading, your go-to question, and always a chance to talk about what you're reading, show off your knowledge, inflate your already overinflated ego, the one part of yourself you actually like. As she opens her mouth she says something you're surprised to hear. *Have you heard of James Joyce?* You reply of course you have, and in that instant you panic, and think it can't be so. Is she going to say it? You've read it, twice, and wear it like a badge of honour, but didn't like it, not even a little, and can't remember anything specific, except maybe a toilet, maybe in the first scene. Everyone liked it but you, you just don't get it. You've always worried that you missed something, that the book is a joke everyone but you is in on. That life is a joke everyone but you is in on. And now you're doubly worried; your number one fear is about to be confirmed. That your number one fear revolves around books says a lot about who you are as a person, but that's a discussion for another time. That's a web for a more sober you to untangle, a bridge for a more sober you to cross.

Time slows down even before she confirms your worst fears: *Ulysses*. Your nemesis. You tell her you're amazed, when in reality you're horrified – story of your life. You ask her why, and she can't answer, simply saying she's reading it because she is, the tautology shocking you. You of course tell her you've read it

twice, something you've probably told everyone you've ever met,
something you're proud of, and reluctantly admit you didn't like
it. She doesn't seem to be affected by this and in this moment
you almost love her. Love again, fuck. You can't stop yourself. In
order not to dwell you move on. Has she read *Dubliners*? Same
author, but a book you actually understand and can talk about
without sounding, or at least feeling, like a fraud. She has, and
you're relieved because you actually liked that book. She asks
you what you're reading. *The Informers. The Informant? No, The
Informers.* You have it in your bag under the table and you get
it out, for clarification. And because it's good to have a prop.
That's the reason you drink so much. Well, one of the reasons
anyway. One of the many, many reasons. The reason you like
to tell people because it sounds reasonable, much more appro-
priate than because alcohol numbs the pain, makes life bearable.
She recognises the name, Bret Easton Ellis, and this is when you
know. A light goes on in your head, and you know what's coming. She asks you what your favourite book is, and you know
this is the end. This question starts you down a path, one that
you know you shouldn't walk, but you're drunk, and you want
to walk down that path and so you do. Has she read *Glamorama*?
She says no, and this is your cue. This is where you come into
your own.

Sometime later, when you have finally stopped talking (ranting)
about *Glamorama* and its effect on your life, the conversation
moves on. She notices your tattoos, another topic you're always
willing to talk about, and begins to ask about them. What are
they of? Stuff, things, nothing particular but nothing not too specific. What do they mean? Nothing, really, you just wanted them
doing and so you got them done. Do you have any others? One
on your chest and one on your wrist. What's on your chest?
Another something, another stuff. Can she see it? Sorry, but as
much as you want her to see you without clothes on, you're not
in the habit of stripping down in pubs, in public. You tell her
to Google the design and she says she will, though you think
she probably won't. Does it matter if she doesn't? Of course not.

None of this does. You're just two tiny organisms on a planet spinning towards its own inevitable destruction. Might as well try to get laid first though.

What's on your wrist? The cross-examination continues. You show her, more ink, more design. Does this have any meaning? Not originally, but now it does. You know it is the worst tattoo ever, you openly offer this description, but that is not what it really is. What it really is is a reminder, a scar from a different time in your life, a time when it was the right idea. Do you regret it? Not at all. Eleven years later, it's not what it once was, but it's still significant. You tell her you don't have any regrets, at least try not to anyway. What's the point in regrets? What purpose do they serve other than to waste time? She doesn't have an answer to this and you're perversely satisfied, though you know you shouldn't be. Fuck it. Once you finally stop talking she says she has none (tattoos, that is), she wants some, but is scared of regretting them later. You tell her that makes sense, but it's not how you view it. You motion again to your wrist, how even though it is terrible, it's a constant reminder of a time when it mattered, and even if it doesn't matter anymore, you know it once did. It's probably drunk bravado but she understands your words, accepts them and says she's going to do it, she's going to get a tattoo. You smile. She smiles.

Eventually, the four of you are outside, smoking, and it's time to call it a night. She's made a note on her phone that she will read *Glamorama*, and this seems the perfect opportunity to do what you shouldn't do but definitely are going to do anyway. You tell her the two of you must discuss it once she's done and ask for her number. She says yes, and you know this is it. You've never believed in fate, in God, in any kind of a reason, but in the space of a few hours you have learned to believe in soulmates. You say goodnight. And then she goes home with one of the other men there. They were together all along. Of course.

Dread. Dread. Dread. It's a dread so strong it feels telepathic. Can you make others dread? You think so. You think you probably could. But you do not. This is your dread, and yours alone. You do not revel in it. Very much the opposite. You do not believe a problem shared is a problem halved. Dread shared is dread doubled. Dread. Hello old friend.

Saturday is just one big hangover – but then again when is it not? You know where you are, at home, in your own bed, alone, but it still feels unfamiliar. You've only lived there a few weeks. Maybe this is why it's unfamiliar. Maybe it's something else. Maybe it's the hangover, the sense of not belonging, of being out of place. This is not a new feeling; in fact, this is an almost constant feeling that mostly manifests itself as an unknowable dread. You reach for your phone and check the time, see that it's early, far too early. The sun is shining in, you forgot to shut the blinds again, but it's too hot to bury your head under the duvet and so you lie there. You need a drink, but when you look to where you would normally put one, the one thing you manage to do anymore that seems vaguely responsible and not out of necessity, all you see is an upturned glass and a pool of water. A legacy of your drunkenness. Instead of cleaning it up, you roll over and attempt more sleep, even though you know this is never going to happen. You lie there for an indeterminate amount of time before giving in and getting up.

You walk to the bathroom, urinate, look at yourself in the mirror. Red eyes? Check. Hair askew? Check. Stubble? Check. Failure to recognise the person looking back at you? Check. These are the signs it is Saturday; you know this because this is how it is every Saturday. You walk back into the one room you live in – the studio to give it its proper name – and take out some underwear. Last night must have been a special kind of drunk, as you slept naked, which you never do sober – you never normally do it drunk either, only when you're especially drunk, undressing in the night without remembering it. You look under the sink at your stash, if it can even be called this, the green herbs that are very much not oregano, and think, today? Not likely. The stash whose contents you cannot allow to be seen or smelled by anyone, whose contents you haven't used in far too long, whose contents for a time formed the very essence of your existence, and wonder when you will be able to consume them. Nowhere in the near future, you think, and the thought depresses you.

You sit on the couch, pick up your phone, sigh and start – first stop is the checks. You check your texts, calls, WhatsApp, Facebook messages, tweets, anything social where you could have said or done anything stupid. Formerly a regular occurrence, the instances are becoming fewer and further between, but this doesn't mean they don't happen. They definitely still happen. A good start – nothing bad here. You look through your phonebook, and see it's not a dream. Eloise Dunhill. You asked for her second name under the pretence of neatness in your phonebook, when in reality it's to stalk her. Not literally, but to look her up on social media, see what she says, what she does, to look at pictures of her and imagine a life together. Digital stalking, 21st-century stalking. Does everyone do it? You don't know. Do you tell yourself everyone does to make yourself feel better? A stupid question that has an answer so obvious it doesn't even bear uttering.

Digital stalking – this is what you proceed to do. You find her easily enough on Facebook; everyone can be found easily enough on Facebook. Privacy? Sorry, don't know what you mean. She is as you remember her: beautiful. No, not beautiful; otherworldly. She's a goddess amongst mere mortals, 1,000 ships launching because of her face. Her profile isn't entirely private, so you look through her posts. It's all the usual; selfie here, self-indulgent status there, omgiloveyouguys pictures left, right and centre. In fact, her profile is plastered with pictures – is she ever not partying? She seems ridiculously popular too. Or maybe that's just the standard level of popularity, you've just been wrapped up in your own life so much that you no longer even know. She has far more friends than any normal person should have. Is she a modern-day socialite? Last night, you thought she was your soulmate, this morning you are not so sure. You thought she was like you, but she is not, she is just another person. You arrogant cunt.

You know you are just like everyone else, even though you try to deny it. You may be less like them than others, but you are not unlike them. Your Facebook may have no pictures, no statuses, only two friends, but you still have a Facebook. Not having an Instagram doesn't make you a revolutionary, it puts you in the second of two categories. Real original. You tweet, while not massively, more than enough. Why you think you're different is that you do not care about these things. Your Facebook is to do what you have been doing; to look at pretty girls. You do not use it, or Instagram, or Twitter, for their proper purpose: attention. You have a practised apathy, a shell, that others do not. You wear it like a badge of honour, and even though it is not, this is how you use it. It's the alienation that confuses you the most, but after twenty-six years you've given up on trying to understand, and you simply accept. You spend the requisite time looking at Eloise, not reading anything about her, simply finding a picture of her, only her, in which she looks fantastic (so, basically, any of them), and stare, pretending to know her, imagining things you shouldn't about someone else's girlfriend, before locking your phone, putting it down and facing the day.

First is the workout, the one you didn't do last night, and do not want to do this morning, but resign yourself to doing anyway. Arms, shoulders, back, chest, legs, you do enough until you ache and you're shaking, and you collapse on the couch. You hurt, more than you would like to at this time on a Saturday morning, but at least it's done, and as an added bonus you've sweated out the hangover. Why do you work out? A question you can't answer. To look good? Maybe. For your health? Fuck that. If you cared about your health you'd drink less and smoke less. Ha. Good one.

You drink juice, a lot of juice, to replace the sweat and alcohol, and for a time almost feel human. As close to human as you ever feel, which isn't much. Next you shower, washing the surface dirt away, and once you've dried and dressed you feel like you might actually make it through the day after all. Which is good, because there are things you need to do. With a sigh, you set about doing them.

Today's outfit: black jeans (standard), plain yellow tee shirt (you try to avoid wearing logos, designs, anything that would give people a reason to look at you), plain blue Vans, checked shirt because it looks a little chilly out. You grab your bag, out of habit more than need, and head out of your flat. You live on the twenty-sixth floor, a building you can't really afford but moved into anyway, your old flat was much more expensive, but you couldn't maintain it once your flatmate moved in with his girl-friend, something you still find slightly repulsive. The notion of spending all your time with someone is an alien concept, a fairly disgusting concept – how could there be someone you want to spend every waking second with? For you, there couldn't be.

The wait for the lift is always a drag, but something you must do; your exercise routine is very new, not yet established enough to entail walking up and down twenty-six flights of stairs. And even if it was, who has the time? Life is short, the amount of time you have to get fucked up is already limited, so you don't want to waste it. While you wait you look out of the floor-to-ceiling windows, across the city. Your city. Not your city from birth, but the one you have adopted. The one you have lived in for more than half a decade, for almost your entire adult life. Leeds. Home to the young. Home to the brave and the beautiful. Home to hopes and dreams that will never be realised. Home to just another set of people. It's beautiful from afar, from a height, from a distance. At ground level it has its moments, but it's nothing special. Just another city.

The lift dings (you don't hear it, by this time you have your headphones in, drowning out the world) and you climb in, press-ing the button for floor one. There are two entrances to the building, however the ground floor has a permanent concierge, who you just don't feel like seeing today. Human contact feels like far too much effort, more than you possess even on the best of days, let alone today. You sway in the lift; you're usually sway-ing on a Saturday morning, the after-effects of a large consump-tion of alcohol, and a lack of consumption of food, the night before. You sway as the lift descends, and after what feels like an eternity the doors open, and you sway out of it. A right turn, through a door, a left turn, and you're outside in the world. Fuck.

It is a little chilly, and so you feel vindicated for putting the shirt on earlier. A small victory, one you'll take, despite it being over literally nothing. There's a slight rain, but if anything this is refreshing, and as you walk the drops hit you in the face, lightly, and you embrace them. You cross the three roads immediately outside your building, gliding through traffic stopped by red lights, feeling superior to the stationary hunks of metal, and walk under the train tracks, through the tunnel, past the same homeless person you see every day, the same homeless person you ignore every day. He has a dog, as if that's not enough reason to ignore him – it's nothing personal, you ignore everyone unless you have a direct need to acknowledge them. You walk to the next set of traffic lights, and cross. Always crossing, it feels like everything is a road, everything is an obstacle to surmount. At the next road you're equidistant between the two nearest crossings, so you just walk across it, taking advantage of the early time, and lack of traffic. Look at you, king of the world.

There are a lot of people around; Saturday in the city centre, and everyone is getting their jobs done, just like you. Just like you. Generally, there are three groups you lump people into: groups of girls, groups of boys and couples/families. The couples are the worst, holding hands, kissing at every opportunity, flaunting their love to the world, acting like they've found the answer while everyone else is still floundering just trying to decode the question. You try not to give them the attention they so badly want, but you can't help it. You're as fascinated with human beings as every other human being is, and more often than not you can't help but stare. Not as bad as the couples, but nearly as bad, are the groups of girls. They are attention all over, and it makes you want to vomit. Everything is a selfie, everything is a tweet or an Instagram, a re-gram or a Tumblr. You rarely drink hot drinks and for this you are thankful, because if you wanted to go to Starbucks for a coffee this would be a life-ruiner. Groups of teenage girls in Starbucks, not because they want to be there, but because they want people to know they are there. Every drink is a picture, every visit a check-in, when you see a group of these girls you don't even stare, you simply look away and move on.

Groups of boys are bad, but in a less obvious way. You're walking through town in jeans and a shirt because you're fairly cold, but the boys are not. Shorts and vests, muscles everywhere. Your favourite (or least, depending on how sarcastic you're feeling) are the low-cut tops, the V-necks that almost go to the groin, in a desperate attempt to show off a chest piece. Pecs and biceps dominate their every move. The social media updates are less, fewer, and for this you're thankful, but only because you're more often treated to the live show. Bitter? Who, you? Not a chance. Anyway, moving swiftly on...

Families you can stomach, but only because families are families; the good ones are interested in being families, not in what you think of them. The bad ones tend not to work, to have jobs, so avoid the city centre on Saturdays, as they can go any day of the week. You feel horrible for being so judgemental, but it's only momentary – and even if it isn't, fuck it. Who cares? The feelings are wind, they flash across you for a second and are gone as quickly as they arrive, invisible, unknown.

You're tired and hungry and hungover and all you want to do is get your jobs done quietly, unnoticed, with minimal fuss, you're not the star of the show, you're not the star of any show, you just want to survive. And so you do. In a fashion.

Your trip to the bank is entirely unremarkable; you change your address, you close an account you don't use and that annoys you when it appears on your mobile banking for some reason, you make small talk with a man you know you'll never see again. The next few shops you go into are as unremarkable as the bank; you buy the Blu-ray of a film of a book you've read, you look at games but realise you own them all, you're not interested anyway, you look at girls but not very much, trying to avoid it mostly, thinking about Eloise. She's become all you are, in your head at least, she embodies all that you want in a person, almost all that you want to be. The very ideal of love, that one thing you've had before, that was ripped away, the one thing you truly yearn for, despite your outward protestations otherwise. That love was not the only love, there were others before, there have been others since, but it was the love. It was the love you've been told all your life you should want, and have, and it will be all you need. You've been tricked by Hollywood, by the cinema and your TV, you've completely fallen for everything they've told you. You've tried not to, but you're a simple man, you're not so complex and different from everyone else, like you're so determined to be. You're a simple man, with a simple need.

You're out of your flat for an hour, two at the most, yet when you return home you feel as if you never left in the first place. You're too new to the place to feel any sort of cabin fever, but you know it's on the horizon, you know one day you and it will be fast friends. But for now, you cope. Upon arriving home you take off your shirt, the day may be cool but your flat isn't, the only window that it is possible to open does not work, heat rising from twenty-five floors below you, most of it passing through on its way upwards, a lot of it staying. Your flat is an oven, and when you're this hungover it really doesn't sit well. You take off your jeans and put on a pair of shorts, you sit on the couch and wonder how to spend your day.

You think the day will mostly be sitting around, thinking, doing nothing, and this is how you know it will pan out, it always does, and today is no exception. You sit, you watch TV, you play games without really paying attention, you pass the time until it becomes a social hour – social meaning of course an acceptable time to drink again. Once it becomes such a time, early evening, around seven, you're thinking what to do when your phone goes off. A text, from your old flatmate. What are you doing tonight? Nothing, you reply, did you have something in mind? He says he thought he could come round, see your new flat, and you agree. He says he'll be there at half past nine, which works for you, gives you time to tidy up, and this is what you do. Wash the dirty pots, quickly vacuum, head downstairs to the shop and buy a case of beer for the two of you to drink. There's no doubt in your mind that, of the ten beers, the split will be at least eight to two, and this is fine by you. You unload the beer into the fridge, and of course promptly open one and have it accompany you to the couch. You wonder what else the evening will hold, your flatmate doesn't particularly enjoy going out, he's very settled with his girlfriend, but you're not, you like to go out. As much as people annoy you, you mostly need to be around them, in order to feel like one. You spend so much time thinking this world might not be real, you might not be real, that you need to spend time around other humans to assure yourself it is, you are.

Your ex-flatmate arrives on time, for him anyway, which is around fifteen minutes later than he said it would be. He's very much like you, and this is why you two get along so well – although you're never late, don't see a need for it. He tries to be mostly invisible, just like you; he barely uses Facebook, never tweets, you know he uses Instagram but you're sure it's only to look at other people, not to post pictures of himself. He doesn't drink or do drugs a lot like you do, but then again most people you know your own age don't, they're more responsible than that. Or at least have better self-control. You're not. And you don't. One day, you keep telling yourself, one day when you meet someone special who will make you a better person, then you'll actively try. Until then, what's the point?

You're fairly certain you met that person last night, but as long as she's with someone else, it's not going to happen. So what does it even matter? What does anything matter? Your ex-flatmate enters the flat and you show him around. It doesn't take long, the place is tiny. You offer him a beer and he accepts, a rare but welcome occasion – it's nice to not be the only person drinking. He sits on the couch, you pull up a chair, the two of you never comfortable sitting next to each other when you don't have to. You're both that kind of person; it's not homophobia, nothing like that, just a simple need to preserve your own personal space. You play some games, all the time talking, catching up, you haven't seen each other for a few weeks since your living split, this is rare, so you have much to talk about. You drink a few beers while he nurtures the first, you knew it would be this way, you don't mind, more for you. Eventually he mentions heading home, it's late, around midnight, he has stuff to do the following day. You dissuade him from this, mention going out, why not go meet his girlfriend and her friends? He's reluctant at first, but you're persistent, you always are when there's a chance to get drunk or high, and eventually he relents, agrees, and you two head out. Into the night, into the world.

There are people all over, there always are in the city centre on a Saturday night. You're heading for the gay district, not as a matter of course, but because that's where your flatmate's girlfriend is, with her friends. She's with a girl you once liked, at least had an interest in, but she wasn't the one for you. She was one of them, not the kind of girl you could see yourself with. At least once the initial fantasies were cast aside in favour of the concept of her as a real person. She denied you, as they are all wont to do, and you moved on with your life. You walk up the street, criss-crossing the path to avoid other drunks; you're drunk by now, a pack of ten beers split nine to one between you and your ex-flatmate. You avoid the shouters, the leerers, the leechers begging for a cigarette. You light one yourself and take a drag, a second, savouring the taste, enjoying how it mixes with the beer and drunkenness, telling yourself you'll quit one day, knowing you most likely never will, cigarettes will be the death of you. Your ex-flatmate is quiet, he's not a night owl, at least not an outdoors one anyway. He'll stay up late, but preferably inside, away from these types, the drunks, it's not his scene. You make it to the club. There isn't a queue, which doesn't bode well, but it's a gay club anyway so you're not exactly looking to meet women, and even if you do happen upon a woman who piques your interest, it won't be Eloise. She's gone, you're best off forgetting her. But you don't want to, will purposely try not to, as you have with so many women. You will torture yourself for as long as you're able, for no other reason than you think that feeling sad is better than feeling nothing.

You want to enter the club but a drunk is arguing with the bouncer, who's telling the drunk he can't come in. The drunk asks why, and the bouncer says it's because he keeps groping lesbians. You watch a back and forth, not really interested, simply waiting, until eventually for some reason the bouncer relents and lets the drunk in. You wonder what the lesbians will think. The bouncer turns to you and your flatmate and lets you in, no problem. There's no entry fee, which is always a bonus, and the two of you walk into a wall of noise, sweat and bodies.

Even in here, where you thought it would be safe, it isn't. You see phones in hands, in front of faces, flashes going off in all directions, brand new selfies, photos no one needs to see, that shouldn't be taken, being taken nonetheless. The world will swell by an unknown number of new, unnecessary photos this night, and though most, if not all, will be deleted, they'll never truly disappear. They'll leave a trace of themselves, they'll haunt the world like so many forgotten ghosts. You ignore them, you have to otherwise they'll overwhelm you, and you head to the bar. A beer for you, cider for your ex-flatmate. The usual, in a way. He claims no cash so you pay but it's not an issue, this isn't a penny-counting friendship, more often than not you're happy just to have someone to drink with. It's always a pleasant change from drinking alone, which is so often the norm. Not that drinking alone is unpleasant, it just happens so often that every now and then you try to break the routine up by drinking with others.

The drinks come, served by someone who might be a male or might be a female, dressed as a male or maybe a female. It's not something you're particularly interested in, so you don't particularly try to figure it out. You turn round to hand the cider over and are met with a giant grin, belonging to the ex-flatmate's girlfriend.

She's an interesting girl, not your favourite in the world but you like her. She's unlike the others, more like you and the ex-flatmate, which is probably why she and the ex-flatmate get along so well, you think. She screams hello, partially due to her being one of the drunks, partially due to the pounding dance music blaring from unknown speakers, in unknown locations. You say hi back and that's about it, you're sure there's more that could be

said but this isn't the time, besides you're drunk and not feeling
eloquent, so you nod along to whatever she's saying, not hearing
her words, not trying to. She entertains herself more often than
not, and you're happy to humour her, she's basically harmless.
You look around, as you often do in clubs, pretending to be taking it all in, but rather just needing something to do, not wanting
to make eye contact with anyone for too long, hoping you're not
leering. You know this is a safe place for women, and you don't
want to ruin it by being just another man. You chain-smoke too
– just another thing to do, another distraction to take you away
from how awkward you feel. This club allows smoking inside for
some reason, and though you know it probably shouldn't, you
don't question it, as it works in your favour. The ex-flatmate's
girlfriend's friends have arrived and they regard you with disdain.
You could wonder why, but you don't bother. They're not really
on your radar, particularly so when they all start taking selfies,
posing and doing hair and make-up and so many other things in
which you're simply not interested.

You dig around in your pockets, looking for cigarettes that
drunk you struggles to locate, doing so eventually, lighting one.
By the time you look up the ex-flatmate and his girlfriend have
gone, disappeared from your view, taken her friends with them,
and while this should bother you it doesn't, your main concern is whether to get another beer, wondering how many people in here have drugs, thinking you could score quite easily
but not wanting to, not trusting what you might be putting in
your body. You realise you're standing nowhere in the club, in
the middle, by yourself, and suddenly you feel conspicuous. You
know very few people are aware of you, the ones who are paying no attention, but you're aware of yourself, aware of being in
the spotlight, aware of being alone. Your drunken mind embraces
the loneliness, as it always does when you're out, surrounded by
bodies, and suddenly you want to go home. You notice you've
finished your beer, and so you drop the cigarette, crush what's
left of it under your foot and quickly leave.

Back outside, the drunk is arguing with the bouncers again,

and you wonder why they're bothering, why any of them bother. Why does anyone ever bother? Alone on the streets now, early hours, you don't know what time but guess around one, you become a target. Drunks in groups love to pay attention to loners, but you don't mind. You have one cigarette left and you light it, throwing the now empty packet in the nearest bin, slightly relieved that the next time you deny someone a cigarette you won't be lying when you say you have none left. All of a sudden you're hungry, though whether you're actually hungry or drunk hungry you don't know, don't care. Though you have cash in your wallet you go to a machine anyway, fumble your card in, enter the wrong pin five, six times until you give up, accepting that the money in your wallet will do. You locate the nearest takeaway and duck in, hoping not to be noticed by the hordes of hungry drunks, shouting at the owner because the pizza they ordered less than a minute ago isn't ready. You order some food and don't question that it appears almost instantly, instead taking it gratefully and stepping outside, away from the madness. You wonder how many takeaways will end up on the internet tonight, how many people think that other people care what they're eating, how many people like other people's food hoping for reciprocation, how much time that could be spent with friends, lovers, spent doing something great, spent changing the world, will be wasted bragging about nothing online. You stumble home, food in hand, eating it quickly upon arrival before crashing out, glad to finally be in bed.

You remember watching TV, the news, and this was recently, not too long ago, it was a morning, a Thursday, and you were ready for work but it was too early to leave and so you were sitting on the couch half watching TV. Terrible things were happening in the world, various countries were bombing other countries, violating international laws, murdering their own citizens as well as those of the other countries, but this was nothing new, and so you didn't really pay attention, until a bulletin about the latest charity fad, people all over the world dumping buckets of ice and water over their heads, somehow this would help seriously ill people, and it had been all over Face-book and Twitter and YouTube and all the other sites you had to be on to be important, and you'd tried to ignore it and it had been hard, but you'd mostly been successful, you'd managed not to watch a single video, but now here it was on the news, the actual news, and they were showing videos, and for some reason you didn't change the channel.

They were saying that millions had been raised for charity, and though you hated the fad, you knew this was good, a spokesman saying they could fund full projects for three years, important research, save lives. They showed someone with the disease, they communicated through a computer with their eyes saying how awful it was, and it looked awful, you felt sorry for him, and then you wanted to turn the TV off because it was making you sad, you didn't want to arrive at work sad and have it ruin your day, but just before you turned it off you heard one of the presenters say that fewer than one in ten people who had taken part in the fad had donated any money, nine out of ten had done it for the sake of it, done it to be seen doing it, and this was when you knew that it wasn't disease, or famine, or anything natural; it is humans that are the real cancer on the world.

Sunday starts with a vibration, your phone is waking you up. You're sure it can't be your alarm, the alarm is set Monday to Friday so there's no reason it would be going off today – unless today is Monday? It shouldn't be but might be, after a certain point the days all bleed into one, nothing with enough significance happens to make the days worth differentiating. You look to the floor, next to your bed, where your phone usually is, but you can't see it. You sit up in a panic; you've lost phones before, not often, but enough for it to be an issue. But this is different. Your new flat doesn't have the internet yet, your phone is your only point of contact with the outside world. You get out of bed, begin to look around. You try to remember what you did with it last night but can't – you never can – so you search. The cof-fee table next to the couch; not there. On the couch; nope. Under-neath the couch cushions, which you unceremoniously rip off; not there either. You locate your jeans from last night, strangely delicately placed across the back of a dining chair; all the pockets are empty. Your panic intensifies, but with the effort of being upright so does your hangover. You get back into bed, take a sip of your drink, which thankfully is next to your bed, where it should be, and try to assess the situation logically. Ha ha, good one.

The juice helps; your throat feels less ragged, your headache subsides a tiny bit (probably a placebo effect but you accept it nonetheless), you feel less groggy. You know your phone must be in the flat somewhere; you've heard the evidence. And right now it's not entirely vital. You glance at the clock on the oven from where you lie, it reads nine minutes past eleven in the morning. Later than you usually sleep in, but by no means a problem – you have no plans, as ever – and so you lie back down. As you stretch your arms out beneath the pillows, your preferred sleeping method, reminiscent of the cats you grew up with, those champions of comfort and laziness, you feel your hand hit something. You lift the pillows up and there the culprit is: your phone.

You press the one button at the bottom centre of it, and see that it was a text that woke you up. You squint at the name, glasses not yet on, eyes sore, and see two words you never expected to: Eloise Dunhill. Your heart begins to pound as you read the four words over and over again: *Hey how are you?* You notice there's no X at the end, but after all this girl is with someone else, why would she give you an X? Hey how are you? Four simple words that change your entire day. You want to reply immediately, but know that you can't. That kind of behaviour doesn't work, apparently, according to friends you've talked to. You're normally a text-back-straight-away kind of man, but not this time. This time you will play their stupid games, and so you make sure the text is marked as read, and then close it. Of course you're forming replies in your head all the time. Hi, I'm good thanks, how are you? Hey, not bad ta, and you? Yo, OK, you? The last one never a real option, far too cool, and most unlike you, but you have to cover every angle. Your head starts to spin, but not because of the hangover. For a change. As is your personality, you start to imagine things. You imagine hanging out with her, talking to her and learning about her and making her smile that beautiful smile some more. The thought fills you with joy, spurs you out of bed, and you ignore the hangover and start your day.

No exercising today; you know you probably should but after two heavy nights you're incredibly tired, your entire body aches and you just don't feel like it. Instead you put the TV on, some rubbish but watchable programme about the police, checking the TV guide you see programmes you want to watch but not until later, a few hours of watching the police will do. No internet means no Netflix, which is appalling but not optional, and so you do as you do with so many other things, and live with it. What's on actual TV is not exactly riveting entertainment, but it provides sufficient background noise, moving pictures you see out of the corner of your eye that entertain you, reassure you, distract you. So much of life is spent waiting, watching screens while watching time pass, so much time spent doing so very little. It's become a part of your condition, a part of you, of who you are. You're not entirely happy with it, but too lazy to change it.

You go through the standard hungover phone checks, same as yesterday, same as most days. As with yesterday, nothing. No texts, no WhatsApps, nothing on Twitter, no new Instagram account, no Facebook messages. This makes you feel better; drunk messaging may have been a real problem of yours before, and though you still check daily to ensure nothing has happened (has happened? Implies natural occurrence. Nothing you've done. Take some ownership of your problems for once), recently you seem to mostly have a handle on it, and when they do come they are tamer, no more solicitous requests, no more declarations of love. You stick around on Facebook, check her profile. No new selfies, which both pleases and disappoints you. You're glad she isn't that frequent with them, but disappointed you don't have more to look at. You browse Twitter, reading through interesting news from external sources, skipping over the selfies and self-congratulatory posts from people who you don't really like, don't know anymore, really have no interest in. All these things pass the time, not a lot of it but some, just enough, so you can head back to your texts and begin to formulate a reply.

This shouldn't be such an issue, but sadly shouldn't and isn't are two very different things. What might she want from you? She must be in contact for personal gain. She must need you to do something for her. And knowing your nature, you already know you will do it. But you don't know how to play it, how to respond. You know you should be aloof, this is someone else's girl, and you have priors with other people's girls that you're not particularly proud of, but as usual you don't want to. You hate the idea of trying to define yourself in writing, of limiting characters that limit your character. As usual, the selfish side of you wants to take over, and you have to fight to stop it. *Hi, I'm not bad thanks, how are you?* A nice neutral reply, not too friendly, not too cold. It's generic, but that's not always a bad thing, you reason with yourself. You press send and immediately lock your phone, put it on the coffee table, get up and take a shower. You want nothing more than to sit with the phone in your hand, praying for it to go off, but it won't do you any good. You could waste your life doing that, you have previously wasted your life doing that, and you're not willing to do that anymore. Instead you let the warm water hit you in the face, wash away the sins of the previous night, wash the smell of alcohol, tobacco, food off your skin, try to bring you back to life.

You lather, rinse, repeat, as you have so often been advised by shampoo bottles, relics of the reading you did on the toilet as a child, before smartphones were with you always. You sing to yourself quietly, softly humming tunes and speaking words, showering for longer than usual, wanting to postpone the inevitable rush to your phone, wanting to savour the growing excitement, a feeling you feel so rarely anymore, one you miss when you do get a glimpse of it. Eventually you're able to turn the water off, slide the shower door back, grope for a towel and thoroughly dry yourself. You brush your teeth, blood coming from your gums as it always does, you ignore it like you always do. At least it isn't coming from your nose, as has so often been the case. You're relieved that your body is clean, and you wonder if the rest of you ever will be. You're mentally dirty, but you reason with yourself who isn't, what is life but a dirty mental capacity, surely only babies are clean, and then it's only a matter of time. Once your body is dry and your teeth are clean you exit the bathroom, put on clean underwear, clean black jeans, a clean white tee shirt, and sit yourself down on the couch. You reach for your phone with hesitation, your arm moving slowly, the anticipation becoming almost overwhelming, until you see it flash blue. Only a small blue flash, for a split second, tiny, fleeting, but it fills you with hope. This dot means a notification. The notification means contact. It doesn't necessarily mean contact from her, but it could. And right now, the could is all you need in order to be sustained. It's enough. But even so, you drop your hesitation and grab it, unlocking it in one swift movement and opening your messages. It is from her. You check the time. It's a little after midday now, probably time to go out for some food. Her message came at five to twelve, less than two minutes after you sent your reply. This fact, this evidence, allows you to drop all pretences. You can be yourself, you can reply immediately.

I'm good thanks, just bored. That sucks, goes your reply. *I kind of am too. Think I'm going to go into town and get some food.* You press send and put the phone down, walk to the window where you spend so much of your time, look out of it. The view from the twenty-sixth floor is special, the novelty has not yet worn off, and you can't stop yourself from staring from time to time. You can see the city spread out below you, the buildings, the streets, you can see tiny people going about their tiny lives, walking and running and riding and driving towards an inevitable apocalypse, one unknowable, unacknowledgable, one best ignored in order to not melt down entirely, in order to persevere. You drift, your mind is a million miles away, and it's only the vibration in your pocket that brings you back. You take out your phone to reveal another message from her. *That sounds great*, she starts. *I could meet you?* Your heart almost stops, as you try to comprehend. You try to understand what the words could mean, what promise lies behind them. It could be nothing. It could be everything. *Sure*, you say, *what time?* Another almost instantaneous reply: *Whenever you want, I live in town. Me too*, you say. *Nation in twenty minutes?* Her reply: *I'll see you then.*

You change your clothes before you go out. Not so much change, as add to. Black jeans are fine, they're the only non-work trousers you own, so it's not an issue anyway. A white tee shirt is fine too, it's plain, neutral, you can't really go wrong. You pick out a shirt, your favourite, a recent purchase from a shop everyone always seems to be talking about as if it means something somewhere. You apply after-shave, how much you do not know, just a couple of sprays, enough that you smell how men are supposed to smell, your natural odour apparently is no longer attractive, humans have evolved past that, and so artificial help is needed, and then you're out of the door. In the lift, down twenty-six floors, and out of the building. Lather, rinse, repeat, not just limited to showers but basically how life is lived. The day is a nice one, sunny, warm considering it's not long past midday, and you think it's going to be a good one. You stop at the first shop you pass, buy more cigarettes, a pack of gum, the whole transaction feeling a little clichéd. You don't know why, but it just does. So much of life does, if you spent time trying to decode every situation you'd die with nothing achieved, except complete mental breakdown. You wouldn't normally smoke on this sort of occasion, but you know she does, so you don't have to try to pretend to be a better person. There are photographers everywhere, the only people who tend to be up and about this early on a Sunday. They're taking pictures, they always are. When it comes to capturing moments, objects, events, that do not need to be captured, they're the biggest culprits. You look down, away, ignore them as you pass, praying as you always do that you don't happen to fall into any of their pictures. You'll never know if you're successful, and so you try not to care.

The city centre is very empty, of both pedestrian and road traffic. The occasional bus, a rare taxi, some amateur photographers

your only companions. You're OK with this. You walk the fifteen or so minutes to Nation, full name Nation of Shopkeepers,
named from a Napoleon quote, someone once told you. Full hip-
ster chic. You're relieved when you find it's open; it being closed
wasn't a possibility you had previously entertained, but when you
passed its big floor-to-ceiling window and saw no one inside you
panicked, dread became you, didn't want to look a fool in front
of her, you have too much to lose, your brain couldn't handle that
kind of rejection, not like this. You sigh and enter, briefly wondering if you should wait outside but deciding against it, thinking it might seem too desperate. You worry it might also seem
impolite not to, but you enter anyway. Too many small deci-
sions, with too many big impacts. In your head at least. You start
to wonder if everyone dwells on these sorts of things as much as
you do, but immediately stop yourself. That rabbit hole doesn't
need a visit from Alice, not today. Not now.

The place is dead inside, and you're relieved (you also laugh at
what you take to be the irony of this statement). This is a picture
place, usually a photographer or two buzzing around, snapping
away, taking pictures for people to share about things that don't
matter, people who pretend to care, people who don't know what
the real things are. You order a beer at the bar, you pay more
than you would want to but that's because you're a cheapskate,
not because the beer is particularly expensive, but the beer is cold
and refreshing, immediately dulling what little hangover was left,
so it's worth the money. And then you wait.

The wait isn't long, soon enough you see her enter from the
same direction you did. You see her before she sees you, and you
can't help but smile; she's every bit as beautiful as you remember.
Today she's wearing black jeans, rolled up at the ankle, pumps,
no socks, a vest top open at the sides, and a red bra, which again
you can't help but notice. You know you shouldn't, but technically you are a man after all, and some parts of that fact don't
always escape you. You see her scan the place, her eyes eventually coming to rest on you, and your smile grows even bigger
as she smiles at you. She approaches you confidently, as if she's

done this a million times before, momentary panic that she has, but before you know it she's hugging you, and this becomes all that you are. You're initially taken aback, but it doesn't take long to get in to it, put your arms around her and give her a little squeeze. She squeezes back before pulling back, saying hi. You say hi and ask her if she wants a drink, to which she immediately replies a beer please. You're impressed by her decision, by the lack of time it took her to make it, and you order one for her, telling the barmaid to put it on your tab. You've become a tab man all of a sudden, you're really playing the part. Are you a dick, does opening a tab look dickish? You don't want to know. Once the beer arrives you ask her where she'd like to sit and she offers up outside as a possibility, one that you immediately seize upon, knowing this will all go better for you if you can basically chain-smoke, have something in your hand, something in your mouth, something to focus on if things don't go well with her. Even if things do, to have a distraction. Usually desperation comes off you in waves, and if you can cover these waves with nicotine, so much the better. You know that things will go well though. You don't know how you know, you just know you know.

Outside you're seated, the only two in the courtyard, and the conversation comes naturally. You ask her about her Saturday, and she happily tells you. She woke up hungover, exercised, read, not much really. The guy she's with wanted to go out last night but she didn't, so she sent him home, ignored his texts and calls once the drink had taken him. She asks about your Saturday, and you fill her in on the details. When you tell her you went out she says you should have texted her. Should you though? She's very forward, and though it scares you it excites you too. But you don't say this, you would never say this out loud, and instead you say you thought she didn't want to go out and she doesn't say anything, caught in the lie. From the look on her face you think it may not be a lie, there may be something more to it, but this early in the afternoon you don't push it, as much as you want to. You leave the thread unpulled, simply allowing the promise of it to take hold of you, and spur you onward. You talk some more, exchanging the words of the newly met; cautious, probing, flirty, intriguing, two boxers sparring before the real punches start flying. You get another drink, before suggesting food, the original reason for your rendezvous. The way she smiles at this suggestion, as innocent as it is, melts you quite a lot, and as you disappear to get menus you struggle to walk like a human, forgetting form and poise, feeling like Bambi. Feeling her eyes on your back makes it even harder, but still you soldier on.

You return with menus and both decide on food; you, a greasy burger, something that will swallow up entirely what of yesterday's hangover may still be hiding inside you, and also line your stomach for what may be to come. She, a slightly less greasy but still greasy nonetheless burger, and you're again impressed, you like how she doesn't limit herself, how she knows what she wants and doesn't let what others think stop her. People do this so often and it always irritates you, being limited by how you might be perceived by others. Fuck the others, eat and drink and do what you want. Die happy; or at least slightly less unhappy.

You disappear again, go to the bar to order, return with drinks and wait for the food. It comes before long, and when it does you're dismayed. Your first instinct is to pick at your chips, continue talking. Her first instinct is to take a picture, share the meal. You try to ignore the fact she is doing this, even though it annoys every fibre of your being, and before long it stops, she begins to eat and you're thankful. The whole thing hasn't soured you, you're pleased to realise. This kind of action would be enough to turn you off most people, but you're glad it doesn't for her. It's then that you truly know she's different. This won't be like always.

As if you'd let it stop you anyway. What's that line? Beggars can't be choosers? Well you've been begging for a long fucking time. Get real, you think to yourself. You'd take any bone anyone offered you.

The food is good; it always is at Nation, and you both polish off your meals without a complaint. You excuse yourself to the toilet, and ask if she'd like a drink on your way back. She says of course, but no more beer thanks, she's bloated. You agree, and say maybe rum is a good idea, and she smiles, nods, agrees. You get up, make your way to the toilet, knowing that rum is going to take this afternoon places you definitely want it to go.

The bar starts to fill up, before long the two of you are no longer alone, the courtyard is as busy as you'd expect it to be on a sunny Sunday afternoon. You're feeling quite buzzed, and you welcome the feeling, it allows the conversation to flow more than ever. More so, it keeps the hounds at bay, it makes your inevitable doom seem less real, less all-consuming. You find out she's an art student, hoping to become an artist. You ask her what she produces and she immediately gets her phone out, goes to her Instagram account and shows you pictures. Not every picture, not at all, she's careful to make sure of that – you want to know why but at the same time you don't, if she wants to keep some things private then you want them to be private, you want her to have what she wants. You wonder why you didn't stalk her Instagram before, you found her Facebook so easily, but then again you wonder why you do almost everything you do, so there's nothing new there. She paints, mostly, abstract pieces with hints of surrealism, something you can't really wrap your mind around, but you smile and nod and tell her you like them, which is not entirely a lie. She asks you if you have an Instagram account, and looks a little deflated when you say no, but this revelation doesn't do anything to kill the mood. The conversation continues, unabated. The words flow from you both like streams, on which you hope dams are never built.

You only know the time is passing by the shapes of the shadows on the table, and how they change. Moving and flowing as if made of liquid, as if they're alive. The table is now littered with empty glasses, the ashtray threatening to overflow, and when you do look at the time it's nearing evening, nearly six. You have no idea where the time has gone, but you know it's been spent well, so you don't question its quick passage.

You're not hungry, not yet, but you know you should eat again. You ask if she is and she says yes, which surprises you, for reasons you can't explain, so you revise your notion and tell yourself you are hungry. You ask what she fancies, and she hesitates, gives you a look, a look that says she wants to tell you something, a look that tells you you need to know what she might say, but she doesn't say anything, at least not what you hoped she might, and she says she wants Mexican. You know a couple of places but they're not what you have in mind, closer to fast food, and it's as if she reads your mind when she says Mexican, but there isn't really anywhere good in the city. You ask her what she wants to do and she says *I have an idea, follow me.* You ask her what her idea is but she doesn't say anything, simply begins to walk, and so you follow. You light a cigarette, light one for her too, and as she thanks you your eyes meet, and you begin to wonder. She has a man, but is one enough? Does she want more? Are you able to be that more? Is more all she wants? Are you willing to change your mind? Put away your doubts? Be that guy, go ahead with it? All these questions are racing through your mind, so you don't notice where she's leading you, until you realise you're in a supermarket. You're about to ask her what her plans are when she tells you she's an excellent chef, and that sentence seems to prevent any further conversation, seems to answer any questions you were going to ask, wanted to ask, were too afraid to ask.

You follow her around the shop with a basket – the faithful hound, always at her heels – and let her pile it high with items. Chicken, peppers, onions, tortillas, jars of sauces and bottles of condiments, beer, some wine, a bottle of rum, all of it very much to your liking. You queue and pay, and when you're back outside, she turns to you and says tentatively that her housemate will be home, buzzing around, she's a bit of a scrub and will want some food, and she half sings *I don't want no scrubs*, which makes you both laugh, and you immediately get the hint, but ignoring it, playing it cool or so you hope, ask *Shall we head to mine?* She seems grateful for the offer and nods, smiles, and as you begin to walk you feel her closer to you than before, inside your personal space, a place you normally hate having people but you want her, even though you are not sure it's somewhere she should be. She gets her phone out and takes a selfie, another, takes random pictures of random things. She tries to take selfies with you and you reluctantly accept, your need not to be in photos dwarfed by your need to please her. It's amazing how your convictions change at a time like this, how easily your principles are forgotten. You tell yourself everyone is the same, and whether they may or may not be, the words help, and so you can go on. You arrive at your building and, ever the gentleman, you hold the door for her, allow her to enter the lift first. She asks *What floor?* and you say *Twenty-six.* She presses the button, and as the doors close you almost say goodbye to the world, wondering if you will see it again any time soon, hoping you won't. Hoping you'll only see her.

You unlock the front door, allowing her to enter before you, wanting her to see the flat on its own, empty, knowing she'll be impressed, and she is. Everyone always is. You give her a brief tour, before taking the shopping bags and unloading them in the kitchen. The first thing she does is go to the window, look at the view. She likes it, everyone likes it, and before you know it she has her phone out, she's taking pictures. *Instagram?* you ask. *Of course,* is her reply. You let her take as many as she wants, careful to avoid getting in them, not wanting to be seen in the pictures, still not sure if you should be seen with her. After a time she relents, you don't know how many pictures she takes, how many different sites they're uploaded to, you don't really care. At least that's what you tell yourself. You're happy she's got her fill, and now she can turn her attention back to you. Which she does. You start to ask her about the food, cooking, but the fact she is immediately in front of you stops you, makes cooking, food, eating at all, seem irrelevant. What is food compared to her? Surely she's all the nourishment you will ever need. You're standing face to face, looking into each other's eyes. You want to make a move but something's stopping you. It's not the pictures, it's not lack of desire, it's not not knowing how to make a move – the alcohol has taken care of that. It's the other guy. You want to ask,

you're dying to ask, but you don't want to bring him up, ruin
the moment. She takes care of that.

You're still looking into her eyes, she's right in front of you
and you can smell her breath, you can taste it in your mouth. The
electricity between you is real and physical, you can feel it, and
when she leans in to you and kisses you, gently at first, but then
harder, full on the lips, it explodes. You don't even consider not
kissing back, and before you know it your arms are around her,
pulling her in to you, your hands on her waist, her tiny frame
fitting snugly in your hands. Her arms are around your neck, her
hands in your hair, her tongue in your mouth, and you know
that in this moment, this is all that matters. The kiss is passionate,
it's full of want and need, full of promises to be made, promises to
be broken, more important promises that will be kept. Eventually
she pulls away and you crane your neck forward, not wanting it
to stop. When your lips are apart, you find the strength to whisper *What about him?* She looks at you, full of fake innocence, and
simply says, *Who?* You take her to bed.

Afterwards, you're lying on your back with your arm around her and
she's cradled into you and she looks at you and asks if you're OK and
you say you are, you're great, and you ask if she is and she says yes
but with a sigh and you don't believe her. Trying not to panic, you
ask her what's up and she says *Nothing*, but the kind of nothing that
is obviously something, and so you ask again. She again says *Nothing*,
but says she has to go, has something to do, and you say *What about
the food?* and she says *Later, after*, and you think you know what she's
going to do but you don't want, can't face, confirmation and so you
say *OK, when later?* And she says she'll ring you.

She gets up and starts to dress – pants, bra, jeans, top –and you
try to stop yourself but you can't so you ask her what she's going
to do and she looks at you and says *You know*. And you say you
know you do but you need to hear her say it, and she says she's
going to break it off with him. For a second you're calm but then
a well of anger rises up in you, and you know you shouldn't feel
this way because you've just got everything you've ever wanted

for two days but you can't help it and you say *Really, you couldn't have done it before? Don't you care about his feelings?* She says she does and you believe her because she seems so sincere, she seems like she genuinely does care about him, and this angers you even more because how can she, after what the two of you have just done? But you swallow it, not wanting to make a good situation bad. And anyway, you're just as guilty. It takes two to fuck, and you can't lie there and pretend it's not your fault, that you're a better person than she is. So you get up too and dress and she's trying to take pictures of you while you do but you playfully (forcefully) grab her arms and throw her phone on the bed, doing so with a smile so she doesn't know that it's making you even angrier. She kisses you and says she'll call you later and you let her out, watch her walk away, lie back down in bed and release the anger, let it flow out of you, to be replaced with pure joy.

You pick up your phone and check Twitter, seeing if there's any news even though you know there won't be, even though it no longer matters, and as you half-heartedly scroll through the tweets, the meaningless nonsense, you notice a birthday wish to someone's grandmother and you think *Really, you're doing it here?* You want to ask them about it but you know it doesn't matter; you just hope they've wished her a happy birthday in real life and not just in a place she'll never see it. You dwell on the tweet for longer than you should, thinking how futile it all is, wondering how people's sights got shifted so badly, but you catch yourself sinking and stop yourself, put your phone down, head into the kitchen to put away the food that was unloaded but never used, destroying a memento of what came before, of a time before her.

Your phone tells you it's fairly late, nearly ten, but you decide you're not tired, surprisingly not hungry, and so you call a friend whose boyfriend lives nearby and ask her what she's doing. She says *Nothing* and you say *Starbucks?* because you know she won't say no, even if she wanted to, she can't miss an opportunity to be seen in one, and there's one in your building so you say you'll meet her there in ten. You head into the bathroom, splash water on your face, will yourself to be more sober, less drunk – she hates you when you're drunk and you get it, she's been the recipient of well-meaning but stupid, dangerous drunken conversations. She's spent so long as the voice of reason you didn't want to hear, you've tried so hard to ignore, and what's worse is she's always been right; you know you've always been wrong, and you still haven't done anything about it. But these aren't thoughts for now – you're drunk and feeling good, you don't need self-reflection, not now. That will come later.

You leave the flat and arrive at Starbucks at the same time as her, which is a relief because you wouldn't be able to sit there without a drink but you don't know what she likes, wouldn't be able to anticipate her order. You get a hot chocolate, as you always do on the rare occasions you find yourself in a place like this; she orders a venti mocha capa-something or other, something you think probably has too much caffeine for this time on a school night but it doesn't matter. You spent your teenage years trying to understand her behaviour and gave up at zero percent knowledge gained, nothing learned, a lot of time wasted. You grab a table and immediately she's phone out, filters on, letting the world she lives in know where she is, what she's doing. You want to ask her if she's saying she's with you but you know she is, not because you're special but because you're a peripheral figure in her world; she can show her everyday friends that she knows other people, she doesn't rely on them, she has other friends.

When she finally puts her phone away – more drinks on more sites, more likes for more self-esteem – when she finally actually talks to you she asks *Are you OK, what's with the late-night call?* You hesitate, debating what to tell her, your fear that talking breaks magical spells swelling to the surface but you can't help it, this girl has known you for over a decade and you know she'll find out eventually, one way or another, and besides you kind of want to brag and so you do. You tell her about Friday, and meeting Eloise, about the boy, and she sighs as you tell your story because she's all too familiar with your past transgressions, she knows your history well, she knows you've done it all before. You smile at her and tell her you know, you've said before no more but here we are, you want to tell her you're sorry but you can't lie, so you don't. You ask her how she is and she says *Fine, same old, teaching sucks but it pays and I'm not rich enough to buy a house yet.* Same old stuff, different day of the week. It's good to see her; since she got a boyfriend a year or however long ago you don't see her as much as you used to, so it's always nice to catch up, but it's always the same. She's aged, physically, but not mentally. And she's mentally tiring. You talk for a while, mostly to the top of her head as she looks at her phone, she Facebooks and Instagrams and Tumblrs but you don't care, you knew it would be like this, it always has been and it always will be, so you let it happen. You remember the past, you discuss the present, you plan for the future. Not real plans, they never are, but they comfort you both, they help to dispel the potentially paralysing fear, the sense of hopelessness that's so near to becoming overwhelming, so it's good to make them.

Eventually the barista tells you it's closing time and your friend tells you it's late and she has school, teaching to do in the morning, and you joke with her about the future of the children she teaches, not entirely unserious, before finishing up your drink, waiting for her to finish hers, and you make your way out. It's still fairly warm even though it's late, and as you walk through the indoor plaza it's not unpleasant. You know work tomorrow will be hard because you're so tired and you wonder where Eloise is, why she hasn't called yet, if she had sex with him instead of dumping him, but the thoughts are unpleasant so you just live in the moment with your friend, try to ignore them. You're mostly successful, which really is the best you can hope for. Your mind has never been your best friend, so you have to accept whatever little it gives you. You reach your point of separation and you hug, as you always have: her because other people do it and she needs to fit in, you because she always does it and you don't want to disappoint her, it's just easier to acquiesce. As she walks off you feel your phone vibrate and you pull it out of your pocket. It's Eloise, she says hey and asks where you are. You say just getting home and she asks where you've been, what you've been up to, and after you tell her she asks if she can come over, make that food after all.

You tell her it's late and you have work early but she says she's blowing off her classes for you, can't you do the same for her? You tell her maybe, you'll think about it, but to come round anyway. Even if you are going to leave her in the morning – which you know you should, even if you won't – you still want to be with her tonight. Earlier was amazing but not enough; you need to smell and feel her skin more, look into her eyes more, convince yourself she exists more, and so she says she'll be over soon and she'll come straight up and as you get in the lift you sigh, wondering where it's all going, wondering where it'll all end.

She arrives some time later. You don't know how long it's been, only that it's too long, and now it's technically Monday, Sunday has gone to bed and you know you should too but you don't, of course, not while the promise of her is alive. The knock on the door startles you – you'd expected your phone to ring or maybe the intercom – but you get up and let her in and she immediately kisses you, just once, and she's moved on before you even have time to kiss back, to be aware of her presence and what's happening. She shoves a piece of paper in your hand: it's instructions for how to use the intercom, must be from downstairs, which is good because you don't know how. For some reason she's put hashtags all over it so now it reads like instructions written by an angsty teenager but you don't say this, simply thank her for the paper and put it down on the windowsill. You ask her how she is, how it went.

She sighs as she looks at you and says *Do you really want to know?* And you say yes, you do, you need to, and you're not lying because you really do, right now you need to know this more than anything in the world. You need to know she was gentle, kind, that she did it with compassion, you know that even if she didn't it wouldn't change anything, things are what they are, but you still need to know. She tells you it was horrible, he cried, she cried, but she was kind, she let him down gently, and even though he cried and begged her she told him sorry, this is for the best, and they hugged before she left and she said they should stay friends even though they both know they won't. And you're glad of this. And even though you know seeing him tomorrow (today) at work will be awful, awkward, never-ending, you're happy, and you reach out and embrace her, and she lets you.

You kiss again, this time with feeling, this time with passion, not just as a greeting, not just with lust. You think about the food but only briefly; you're hungry but not for food, not any-more. You're holding a hunger that can never be satisfied by eat-ing, probably never be satisfied by anything, but you know that physicality is what it demands, and so that is what you give in to. Before you know it the two of you are in bed again, doing all the things you never thought you'd do yesterday, things that without knowing it you always wanted to do with her, things that make you complete.

When you're done, you can't let her go, you hold on to her as if she's your only connection to this world, and in many ways she is. She doesn't move, doesn't try to get away, and you check the time and it's two in the morning, a Monday morning, and your alarm is going to go off in five and a half hours but the thought doesn't worry you like it normally would; it barely even moves you to care at all. As if she can read your mind, she looks up at you and says *I assume you're not going to work?* It's a statement, not a question, and her assumption annoys you, even though she's probably right, because even now you're entertaining the idea of going in, you know you should, being with her is amazing but it doesn't negate your responsibilities, and when you don't answer she asks again and you sigh and say you have to, it's a work day and you have work to do, money to make and bills to pay. While this is true, right now it seems irrelevant. But isn't that just what life is, an irrelevant truth?

She's not happy, it's written all over her face, but she doesn't get mad, instead of complaining at you she becomes desperate in a way, almost pleading with you not to go. *I'm skipping my classes,* she says, and you acknowledge this and before you can stop yourself you say *I know, but they're just classes* and immediately you know you shouldn't say this. Just because it's not important to you doesn't mean it isn't to her, but she isn't offended, isn't annoyed, she seems to agree, but continues to plead nonetheless. This throws you, but you proceed anyway. It's a back and forth, she's trying to convince you, you're trying to convince her, secretly inside you're trying to convince yourself, and as soon as she starts asking the right questions you know she's going to win. *How long have you worked there?* she asks. *Three months*, you answer, *give or take*. And how many sick days have you taken? *None*, you say, knowing she's already won. Don't you think you're due one? You want to tell her this is not how it works, it's not that simple, but lying here in her arms you know it is this simple, you will do what you can to not move from her for as long as you can. Without answering – it might have been a rhetorical question anyway – you kiss her hard on the lips, no tongue, just pushing your mouth against hers, and when she pushes back you know it's all going to be OK. You kiss for a time beyond counting, a period of your life where everything is fine, world peace and world hunger and the Middle East have all been solved, your kiss has cured the planet, the universe, of all ills, and it's only when you stop kissing that the problems exist again. But they don't matter to you, all that matters is you're here in your bed, lying on your side, and she's pressed in to you, and you have your arms around her and you're holding hands with her and when you squeeze her hands she squeezes back, and you fall asleep and the sleep is everything to you.

There was a girl, you remember her distinctly, she played such a big part in your life. You'd met her through mutual friends, at least in a way. You were friends with her boyfriend, she was friends with your girlfriend, and at the time she was the most beautiful girl in the world. But not just that: she was funny, she made you laugh a lot, she made you feel things, not sexual, not even romantic, she just made you feel. This was everything to you, because so little ever moved you. But she moved you.

The way she moved made you want to move too, and together, not just her, the four of you, you'd taken a lot of drugs, you'd all been to a different place, a special place. You'd all laughed, there had been tears, literally blood and sweat, but it had all been something else, something you'd never experienced anywhere else, something that wouldn't have made sense anywhere but there, at any time but that.

You'd all grown up, not become adults, but grown as people, and she'd broken up with her boyfriend, and you'd broken up with your girlfriend, and your only contact with her was online. You'd talked – nothing special, just words – but then she'd said you should meet up, hang out, and you hadn't even hesitated to say yes. You went round to hers, and she'd cooked for you – vegetarian – then the following night you'd cooked for her. You'd changed your favourite recipe to make it vegetarian, and she'd watched you cook, kind of; in reality she'd been on her phone, she always was, but she enjoyed the food, had eaten it all, and you'd drunk and smoked, and it had been great, and somewhere along the line you ended up sleeping together, which wasn't a good idea, you both knew it, but it couldn't be taken back. And afterwards came the insults, the death threats, it all devolved into something ugly; the mask had been ripped off and what was underneath was more terrifying than you could have possibly imagined. And after that you never really spoke again.

You awake once Sunday has fully segued into Monday and you stretch, glad to see you actually closed the blinds last night for once so it's not too sunny, but then you panic, firstly because you're late for work – late for ringing in sick for work anyway – and secondly you're alone. You scramble for your phone and realise the first issue is OK: even though you've slept through your alarm it's only eight, you don't have to be in until half past and so you have plenty of time to ring in. Not hesitating, needing to deal with the second issue immediately, the lack of Eloise, you ring your boss and put on your best fake sick voice and tell her you have diarrhoea, your go-to excuse for a sick day, one where not sounding too sick isn't an issue, and where follow-up questions are avoided, the lack of investigation welcome on both sides of the conversation. You try to get your boss off the phone quickly so you can call Eloise, find out where she is, but as you're hanging up you hear the front door open and you panic because you don't know who else has keys but as she calls good morning, louder than you'd like at this time, and hear the rustling of shopping bags, you know it's OK, she must have gone to the shop downstairs. The dread recedes, at least for now. You know it'll be back, like clock-work, like the incoming tide, but for now the tide is going out and so you can do your best to ignore it.

You're proven right as she enters, bags in hand, and starts unloading them in the kitchen. In this moment you're the most grateful you've ever been because you're suddenly aware you've not eaten since early yesterday afternoon, your stomach is crying out for some sustenance, so you force yourself to get up and you wrap your arms around her from behind, kiss her on the cheek and quietly say *Thank you.* She says *For what?* And you motion towards the food, and tell her you're starving and to sit down, and that as a thank you you'll make breakfast. She doesn't argue, and as she turns away from the kitchen you kiss her properly, on the lips, thanking her again. You watch her sit on the couch and turn on the TV, some news programme, two people also on a couch talking about all the horrible things happening all over the world, but this doesn't stay on long, and soon it's *The Real Housewives of God knows where* and you turn away, uninterested, and start to make food.

First of all, peeling and squeezing some oranges, juice for you both. This takes a while as you make a pitcher, placing it in the centre of the table, and then you turn your attention towards the meats. Oil in a pan, and once it starts to sizzle you add sausages, frying them until it's time for the bacon, then adding tomatoes, mushrooms, finally putting some bread in the toaster to complete the meal. Once the toast has popped and you've buttered it you turn to place it on the table and see she's no longer watching TV, instead she's facing you, phone in hand, and you smile at her and ask her how long she's been like this, and she doesn't answer, just smiles mischievously, and continues.

You sigh, knowing you'll once again be on the internet, and you begin to feel bad for the guy she's just broken up with. Is he going to see this? Will it crush him? It would crush you, already, at this early stage, to see her with someone else. And beyond him, there will be people you don't know talking about you, judging you, and though it bothers you you brush it aside, the amount it bothers you is much less than your hunger, for food this time, for once, and so you dish out the contents of the frying pan equally, place the two plates on the table and say *voila!* Finally she puts her phone away and this time she kisses you thank you, before taking a seat, you sit next to her, and you eat. You don't talk, she must be as hungry as you are, unless she ate last night with the other guy she hasn't since you did, and between you you polish off all of the food in a scarily short amount of time. You lean back in your chair, full, satisfied, and she's doing the same and you wonder if the two of you are in sync already, wondering if it's possible and assuming it must be as you appear to be. But you dismiss the thought, your mind is clouded by lust, thinking straight isn't a big option right now, you're only thinking Eloise.

At least you're not thinking doom.

Before long she inevitably reaches for her phone and starts to text, message, Instagram, whatever, and you're about to clear up but she tells you to get your phone, to check Facebook. You tell her that even though you have an account you rarely use it, your only friends on there are people who live abroad and who aren't easily contacted in other ways, people who upload pictures you're actually interested in, but she disregards this, tells you she knows but to do it anyway, and so you do. One friend request, before you even open it you know it's from her, and you can see her studying you, watching your face and the movement of your hands, and before you've even reacted she says *Please accept it?*

You don't want to but know it'll be easier if you do, and so you do, another in a long line of instances of you doing something you don't want to because it's the easier option, because there'll be less conflict. You think you know why she wants you to but you don't say anything, simply accepting it before closing the browser and putting your phone down. She's still looking at you, waiting for a reaction, and rather than saying anything you grab her and pull her in to you, holding her face in your hands, and kiss her, knowing this is easier than words (a sentence from a book flashes across your mind – a warning?), knowing even if you could explain to her it wouldn't work, she wouldn't under-stand, and so you say no words, you use your lips in another way, before letting her go and starting to clean up.

After the table is cleared, the dishes washed, the flat is generally tidied, you take it in turns to shower, your shower only being small, which is frustrating, but she promises you her shower is bigger and the promise contains more than the words in the sen-tence and this is what gets you through the shower, what you think will get you through the day. It's the promise of something more, something you can only comprehend in an abstract way until the promise is realised, and the realisation captivates you, consumes you, becomes you. You brush your teeth and dress, waiting for her to do the same, watching her applying make-up, becoming bored with it and watching TV, and while you're watching TV you play around with your phone, logging on to Facebook, wanting to confirm what you knew all along, as soon as she asked you to accept her friend request. You know before you even see the notification, one new request, that it was always going to be this way. Eloise Dunhill wants to be in a relationship with you.

You don't say anything to her, you just watch her. Her phone must vibrate because she puts down her lipstick, about to be applied, and picks it up. Almost immediately she turns to you with a huge grin on her face and practically pounces on you. She tries to kiss you but you stop her, needing to clear things up first. You ask her, *So we're in a relationship now?* She says she wants to be, and so you say *Ask me.* She looks confused, and says *Ask you what?* But you don't explain, instead just say *Ask me* again, and you can see the realisation on her face, and she suddenly looks very solemn and says *Will you be my boyfriend?* You know it's soon, you've known this girl less than three days, but you also know that doesn't matter, social convention rules so much of your life but it shouldn't rule this, and so you say yes, and let her kiss you, and she squeals as she does and you almost do too but you don't, simply smile, and the kiss is awkward, toothy, but only because you're both smiling so much and eventually you're able to kiss properly, like two twenty-somethings, as opposed to two teenagers. You hold her for a while before eventually letting go, her saying she needs to finish getting ready before you go, and you realise that the two of you haven't even discussed where you're going, she might know but you have no idea, but you don't mind, just being where she is will be enough for you.

As you turn back to watch TV your phone vibrates and you take it out, a text from the friend you saw yesterday, and all it says is you're in a relationship?! You knew this was going to happen, you knew this is why your relationship was known to Facebook before it was known to you. You know that Eloise's phone will be blowing up with calls and texts and Facebook messages and tweets and re-grams, you know she'll be basking in the attention, and though it isn't your first choice you know you'll let her, you know this means something to her. You again worry about the guy she has dumped very recently, you find yourself worrying about him a lot. But each time, you also find yourself worrying less. And less. And you know soon not only will you not care, you won't even wonder. And so now, in the present, you force yourself to think about her instead. It isn't hard.

You might be old-fashioned in many ways, including privacy, but she is obviously less so, this will be a compromise, but one that you are more than willing to make. You reply to your friend, saying *Yes, can you believe it?* She asks you if it isn't a little quick and you say *Maybe, but does it really matter?* If you got together today, or got together in two weeks, what would be the difference? She relents, agrees, and says she wants to meet her, and you ask her how she knew anyway and she says mutual friends, one of Eloise's friends messaged her to ask aren't you her friend, and she of course immediately texted you, and here you are. You tell her of course she can meet Eloise, whenever she wants, and she says OK and she'll call you when she's not at work. You don't ask why she's texting when she should be teaching, but you know she lives in a digital world so you give her the benefit of the doubt and don't raise the issue, you know it's not one worth debating, it's an argument with no successful outcome, there's nothing to be gained.

By now Eloise has finished, is ready, and she looks beautiful, devastating, you know she's capable of destroying you, you belong to her now and in a second she could undo your entire existence, and you just pray silently to a God you don't believe in that she won't. You tell her she looks beautiful and she says *Thanks, you look hot too*, and you don't believe her because you don't think much of yourself but you take the compliment, knowing it won't do either of you any good to argue it, and after the two of you embrace she tells you it's time to go. You ask where and she says *To the zoo, of course*, and you wonder why she says of course, where the assumption comes from, should it worry you, but instead you say OK, inside you're filled with trepidation as zoos make you sad, you want the animals to bask in their freedom, but it's a moral quandary you've been through too often, and one that isn't going to come up this early in the relationship and so you say *OK, which one?* She mentions one nearby, one you've successfully managed to avoid going to so far, and she says she'll drive, which is something you didn't know she could do but is good because you don't have a licence, it was taken in an incident that doesn't bear thinking about now, one that happened and will be addressed but not right now, in the unspecified future, and you let her lead, you lock the flat door behind you, follow her into the lift, follow her into the underground car park.

Her car is better than you expected from a student but you don't question it, financials are not to be pried into, you simply let her unlock it and you slip into the passenger seat. She tells you it's a nice day, and you haven't been outside yet today so you take her word for it, and she puts the top down and you know you're going to enjoy the ride. She turns the engine on and it roars in a way you didn't expect and you put on your seatbelt and brace yourself for her to pull away but she doesn't, not right away. Instead she leans over to kiss you and you kiss her back and as you're kissing you hear the click of the camera on her phone and you know she's just taken a picture of the two of you kissing and you pray it won't go online, knowing it will, but before you ask her not to upload it she's pulled away, pulled herself away from you, pulled the car away from the space.

All thoughts of potential questions have been long blown out of your head by the time she's pulled into the car park at the zoo, by the time the car is stationary and the top is coming back up. You both get out of the car and she takes your hand and you walk to the entrance, you pay the fee for both of you and then you're inside, immediately into the dark, some sort of bat cave, the kind you've been in countless times before, but you still feel uncomfortable in. The cave is eerie, the bats fly freely around you and you can feel them touching you, brushing your arms and your hair, and you can feel her hand tense each time one passes by her, you can feel her moving steadily closer in to you until you're practically wearing her. The bats feel like a metaphor but if they are it's one you can't grasp, it's just out of your reach, and so you're forced to let it go. Eventually you emerge out the other side (of the cave? Of the metaphor?), relatively unscathed, and next up are the bugs. Never your favourite part of the place, but she seems entranced, and you sort of hang back each time she approaches a tank, you feign interest as she points out each disgusting tiny creature, you pretend to care as she explains where they're from and what they do.

It isn't too long (though long enough) before the bugs have finished and next it's the garden, heated to an intense degree, butterflies floating everywhere, and though you will none of them to land on you you enjoy watching them fly, they're beautiful, and serene in a way. They emit a peace you know you'll never feel but dream of just the same. As you walk she's almost constantly taking pictures, you pass a mini waterfall and she stops a stranger, asks them to take a picture of the two of you, and you put your arm around her shoulder and smile, not forced as it usually is when you're in pictures, your smile is natural, as natural as the flowers around you, and she thanks the stranger as they move on, she inspects the photo and plays with it, you assume cropping and filtering and uploading, you don't ask, you don't want to know, you already know.

After the garden is the desert, which is merely a large open space with some sand on the floor, a few sad-looking meerkats on their hind legs, protecting their young from an imagined threat. The meerkats bring feelings up in you you've managed to hide up to this point, a sense of being trapped. You've been to various zoos various times before in your life and you've always empathised with the animals, their trappedness is more literal than yours, but you feel a kinship, you feel as if you know their pain. You tell Eloise you're thirsty and pull her quickly along, and soon you find a café, and though it's the end of the incredibly short tour, a lot shorter than you remember, you're glad, and you get a Coke and ask her if she wants one and she says no but then takes yours from you and drinks from it, and you always knew this was going to happen, you always knew it would be this way, somehow deep down inside the unknowable future was always known, it had been written long ago, and had already been revealed to you.

Even though the tour felt short it's lunchtime, the sun is high in the sky and the day is beautiful, and you ask her if she's hungry and she says not yet, instead she asks if you want to get out of the city. All around you there are people taking pictures, pictures of food and drinks and themselves and other people and plants and animals and suddenly there's nothing you want more, it's all too much, the need to leave that you feel is overwhelming, your throat has tightened and you almost can't breathe, the world becomes a blur and you nod frantically and almost run away.

She asks you where you want to go and you mention the nearest city, Manchester, an hour away by road, probably less so in her car, with her driving, and she agrees and you say you just need to go pack a few things and she nods but when you're back in the car she goes in what you think is the wrong direction, heading towards Manchester, rather than back to your place, and you tell her this and she says she knows without looking at you, and you look at her for a long time before eventually looking away, and when you do she looks at you and smiles, that mischievous smile you're fast becoming used to, and speeds up. You light a cigarette and pass it to her, then light another for yourself, and soon the car is flying, you're flying, you can see your building fading away in the car's mirror and it's OK, the direction is fine and all the pictures are fine and you pull out your phone and open the browser then stop, close it again, thinking that you know you're all over her social accounts, you don't need or want confirmation, it will change nothing. You can see her phone lighting up each time a message comes through, it's nestled on top of her bag, but thankfully she doesn't pick it up, not while she's driving, too many people you know do this and it's so worthlessly dangerous that you almost love her merely for the fact she doesn't do it.

You stop at a café for a drink on the way, you smoke some more and talk, lighting cigarette after cigarette and saying word after word, learning about each other, and eventually you reach the new city. You ask her where she wants to stay and she mentions a hotel, way out of your budget, and you're about to say this when she says *It's on me*. You know you should protest but you don't, you let her, and this is a city you've been to before and when she heads in a different direction to the hotel you question her but she says she has to make a stop first, has to see a friend. You don't ask who but she tells you anyway, she has to see a Bolivian, she needs some marching powder. This is not the answer you expected, but it's not one that discourages you. You look at her and think that this girl could turn out to be a lot of fun.

There was a film you saw, on a whim one hungover Sunday afternoon stuck on the couch, you knew the name, and of its reputation, but knew no more. And so you put it on and watched, enthralled, and in the one hundred minutes it played for it consumed you, it inserted itself into your brain and took over all your faculties.

When it finished you sat in disbelief, not sure what you had just witnessed, only knowing it had changed you. You wanted what it offered. You had had it before and lost it, and wanted it again. But better. Perfect. You longed for what was no more. You longed for what might be.

You watched it again later that day. And the next day. You ended up watching it every day for an unknowable length of time, each viewing no more, nor less, than the one before it, the one after, the viewing a hundred times before, or a hundred after. You learned so much about the world sitting on that couch, at least the world as you wanted to know it. You learned so much about yourself, as a person, as an entity, as an abstraction. You forgot who you were and learned again, and though you felt dramatic thinking it, you knew it was true; nothing was ever the same again.

You didn't see Eloise as the type to buy drugs; granted you've only known her for a few days, but she's never mentioned it, none of the pictures you've seen of her have contained any, have seemed to show her on any, but you don't ask, fearing the answer but not knowing why. Excited by the answer too, but again not knowing why. A little while after entering the city you're driving down unfamiliar streets, a posh neighbourhood, probably rich, not the kind of place you've ever bought drugs from. But then again considering the car she drives, the fact she is a student blowing off classes, you guess she and you had run in different circles before, and eventually she turns into a drive, a gate blocking the way, but before either of you do anything the gate opens of its own accord, you can hear the soft hum of the motor as the two doors separate, pulling back. She drives the car up to the house, swinging around the clichéd fountain on the clichéd brick driveway, like something out of a thousand films you've seen, and stops, puts it in neutral, handbrake on, and gets out. For lack of anything else to do you follow her, matching her stride but falling a little behind, knowing you have no reason to be apprehensive but being so anyway. Apprehension, the old friend, never waiting for an invitation, always just around the corner. Eloise rings the bell and a butler appears, a small, old, well-dressed man, and he smiles at Eloise as if he knows her, and without saying anything he steps aside and she walks in.

She walks around the house confidently, knowing where she's going, she turns left and right through doorways and around corners and soon you're lost, hoping that you won't get separated because you're not sure you could find your way back out. Soon she opens a door into a vast room, bright, one wall entirely glass, overlooking the city, another wall a single huge screen, you have no idea how many inches the screen is but it's bigger than any you've ever seen. There are huge green couches in an L shape taking up most of the floor space, what little is visible made up of wooden flooring covered by a shaggy rug, which looks out of place but what do you know? On these couches various people lounge. They all look up as the door opens and say her name almost in a chorus, all of them seeming to brighten up at her presence. A feeling you very much understand, one of the few you do. She says hi and smiles and she introduces you, *This is my boyfriend.* You're initially taken aback by the phrasing before you remember it's true, and you say *Hey* and shake various hands, are given names, immediately forget them, despite your best efforts. On the coffee table are various white powders, bags containing green substances, some syringes, but you don't want to see the syringes so you walk to the glass wall, pretend to be interested in the view, which is actually incredible, just hoping Eloise doesn't plan to stay, hoping she makes a quick transaction so you can leave, get away from the needles, get away from the terror that has been growing inside you and is threatening to explode out of you and take a form you don't want to, can't, imagine.

You stare out the window for what might be a long time, what might be a short time, either way it's as long a time as you can manage before you start to feel awkward, and turn back to see one of the guys offering Eloise a line. You're delighted when she declines, though you don't know why, she says she's here to buy and can't stay. The guy asks how much, and she says how much, an amount not huge but definitely not trivial, definitely noticeable. She hands over the requisite amount of cash, carefully counting the notes from what you now notice to be a bag far grander than anything anyone you know has ever sported. The guy she's transacting with hands over the bag, and much to your relief she's saying bye, taking your hand, leading you back through the maze until you're back out in the open, just the two of you, in her car, safe. You want to ask about the drugs but this isn't the time, not yet, and so you pretend not to care and as she pulls away you ask if you're going to the hotel, and she says yes, and you're relieved.

She turns back through the unfamiliar winding streets, and soon you're back in places you know, streets you recognise, and as she pulls up to the hotel a valet appears as if from nowhere and you worry but the bag is nowhere to be seen, she must have slipped it into her purse effortlessly, like a pro, and she hands over her keys and a twenty, a big tip you think but she doesn't seem bothered, it's nothing compared to what she handed over in the house, and soon you're in the lobby. You approach the check-in desk but you don't check in, instead the person behind the counter greets Eloise as if he's known her for years, and without any sort of transaction hands over a set of keys, and says it's good to see her. She says *You too*, before taking your hand and pulling you to the lift. Once inside, she inserts one of the keys into a slot labelled penthouse and the lift goes into a sort of lockdown mode, it flies directly upwards without stopping, opening at what must be the penthouse in question. The place is incredible, an expanse the likes of which you've never seen, except on TV, the likes of which you've certainly never been in, nor ever thought you would. You look at her and she says *I know you have questions, soon, but first we need to eat, it's going to be a long day, we should have some sustenance*, and as everything she says is right you don't debate any of it, you just let her do what she will.

She asks what you want and you say you don't know, so when she rings room service she orders a big spread, you look at the menu and most of the items have ridiculous prices next to them, and you're so glad she said it's on her, even though you feel bad, you want to contribute. Once again she seems to read your mind and says *It's OK, you can make it up to me*, and you have no idea how you will but you smile and thank her. Her phone rings, and she disappears into another room to answer it. While she's gone the food arrives, and when you open the door a man wheels in a full trolley, he starts to unload it but you tell him not to bother, it looks like it would take an age, and you fish around in your wallet but you only have a ten and the man takes it anyway, trying to look grateful. You're more upset by his reaction than you know you should be; that's a lot of money to you, but to him it seems like nothing. Eloise really does live in a different world, but the feeling soon passes, and you're left with just yourself, he's gone now anyway.

There's all the food you could ever want, but before you eat you go find her, tell her it's here, and she smiles and says bye to the person she's talking to and hangs up. She says she's starving, and skips past you, grabs a burger from the trolley and takes a huge bite. The sight of her doing this is music to your eyes, and you take the burger from her playfully, also taking a bite. She looks at you with mock offence, and soon you're both taking bites, racing through it, before coming to a sort of modern day Lady and the Tramp stand-off. It's fairly horrendous, but so much of life is that the feeling is a common one, it carries no surprise, only familiarity. You let her have the last bite and after you've both swallowed she kisses you, then starts picking at a plate of chips, delicately picking them up between thumb and forefinger and popping them in her mouth with an ease that is juxtaposed with the tightness of her body. But it's a juxtaposition you like, very much indeed.

You let her eat, not as hungry as you were, and you walk over to the window, take in the city. You're so high up, you don't know how many floors, and the view is breath-taking. You can see for miles, the day is still beautiful, the sky is clear, you feel like you can see all the way to your own home from here.

Of course the thought is ridiculous but you entertain it anyway, enjoying the idea. You can feel her eyes on you again but when you turn around you see it's not just her eyes, but the eye of her phone again. She's taking pictures, and you let her, wanting her to feel at home, because you're beginning to suspect this may be her home, one of them at least. Does she have multiple homes? Are her family very wealthy? You pull stupid poses, almost getting into it, only stopping when she stops taking pictures, starts tapping away, and you assume they're being uploaded, more moments captured, more parts of life rendered invincible by virtue of being online. What was it you once read? Something about forever, it being a fortress? Very different context, very much the same message.

You pick at some food while she does this, ignoring the vibrations of your phone in your pocket, not wanting to deal with anyone else right now, knowing nothing that anyone has to say to you can be as important as the fact you're right here with Eloise, and soon she's sitting down in what must be the living room of the suite, lounging on a huge couch, lying down, and you lie next to her and take her in your arms. You look into each other's eyes and kiss softly, full of passion, no want in this kiss but you know it's there, lurking. After the kiss you look at her with what you hope is a quizzical expression, and she sighs and says *I guess you have some questions.* No shit you do, you think to yourself. Who are you, really? *I have a lot to tell you*, she continues, *but first.* And with that she gets up, grabs her purse, pulls out the bag of powder and a twenty. She rolls up the twenty and offers it to you, not saying anything, simply pushing it towards you and raising her eyebrows.

That familiar burn, the sting in your nostrils, the supreme energy and confidence, you haven't felt this in a long time. It isn't long before the coke talk begins, and though it's usually bullshit, this time it's actually interesting, you're actually listening. And listening is all you're doing, because she's practically ranting. *Yeah so you're probably wondering about the hotel well my parents own it well not own it it's sort of like franchised nothing official but basically they put a lot of money into it and take a lot of the profits and they've done this all over the world and the penthouse is owned by them but I don't think they've ever been here except maybe once just after they first got it.* She breathes. *And yeah so I come here a lot it's technically where I live well it's one of my homes I guess my official home is in the States with my parents but I don't really like it there it's too hot and the people are all annoying so I have most of my stuff here but really I spend all my time in my other place near the art school I'm going to near where we met.* She stops talking briefly, another massive line, then more words, she's like a waterfall. *So yeah that's the hotel and that explains the car too and why I don't go to art school very often I mean I know I should but it's hard to see a point in it you know to me the point is looking good, feeling good, people knowing you look and feel good and that's why I'm always photographing you and me and stuff and that's why the drugs too I love my parents don't get me wrong at least I think I do, well I know I should anyway but they're never around and it makes me feel pretty shitty but with this stuff,* she indicates the bag, *with this stuff it kind of doesn't really matter so yeah do you know what I mean?*

You're sort of blown away, you've been pacing to try to dissipate some of the energy but it's not really done anything, you're ridiculously high considering how early it is in the afternoon, and you stop pacing but only for a second to look at her, and you know she wants an answer but none comes to mind, and so you grab her arm and pull her to her feet, to you, and kiss her hard, probably too hard but you're both so coked up it seems the right thing to do. You can feel your erection but this isn't the time, not now, so you let her back down to the floor and take the note from her and do a massive line yourself.

The late afternoon and early evening sort of pass in a haze and before you know it you're out, in the town, wearing the same clothes you've had on all day and you're unshowered since this morning but you don't care, you've got pure confidence in your veins and so the two of you are walking, practically strutting down the street, you have a cigarette but you're not paying it much attention, except to make sure none of the ash goes on your clothes. You come to a bar, The Oyster Bar, not the most fashionable but reasonably discreet, and soon you each have a largely ignored drink in front of you, and while she sits and texts and makes the occasional call you just sit, look around, wanting to go outside, breathe the air, expend some energy, but not wanting to not be by her side. She says some of her friends are coming, she hopes you don't mind, and you say it's chill, it'll be nice to meet some of the people in her life, and because of the drugs she laughs but you actually mean it, you don't want to let this one go, you want to get your hooks into her. You know that's an awful way of phrasing it to yourself but you also know it's true, and so when her friends arrive you pretend not to be high, which you're not really much anymore anyway, you've purposefully not been bumping in order to not make a bad impression. Her friends are just like her: slim, beautiful, phones out, drinks out, but from the looks of them they're not currently reading *Ulysses*; in fact you wonder if they can read at all.

You let them talk, it's mostly about you, Eloise's friends interrogating her about you, but she's ducking questions, trying to avoid the fact she doesn't actually know much about you, and by now the coke has worn off and so you drink your drink, then drink another, and soon you're pretty buzzed off the alcohol. A couple of her friends look familiar, you feel like you've seen them before, but you chalk this up to the alcohol. That sense of familiarity a slight buzz often brings. Is it the alcohol? Do you care? You sense Eloise is buzzed too from the way she's looking at you, lust tinged with desperation, but regardless her phone is out and her friends' phones are out and it's all selfies, group photos, you're dragged into photos by people whose names you don't even know, faces you won't remember, and you're thinking it's all so cheap, this is all so vague and unnecessary, but you let it happen anyway. You know Eloise is like this, you're just glad it's not as much as her friends are.

Soon Eloise is taking your hand and you're outside, leaving the bar, moving on to the next. You light a cigarette for the walk and give one to Eloise but soon all her friends are asking, begging cigarettes from you, and it just seems easier to give them all one and so you do, and they're coughing and looking unsure but they're all so proud of themselves, this small act of drunken rebellion making them feel like better people, even though you know if anything it's the opposite. The next bar is Footage, you've not been here for a while, but nothing much has changed. This bar is more crowded, and despite being drunk you practically beg Eloise and she takes you into the disabled toilet and you do a bump each, two, and once you're back in the room everything seems much easier to handle, it's given a perspective that means something to you, or at least feels like it might. Her friends have attracted a lot of attention but you and Eloise stay on the periphery, not wanting to be antisocial, but not wanting to be involved. Drinks are ordered and drunk, bumps are discreetly done, and soon it's the early hours and you're tired, your nose hurts, your head is spinning, you're dreading tomorrow, dreading your exposure to the world under the influence of such solicitous inebriants. But in reality you're back in the penthouse and it's just you and Eloise, you've managed to kick out her friends, and their new friends, and it's just the two of you and you go to the toilet, to actually use the toilet for a change, and when you come back Eloise has left the living room. You head for the bedroom and find her standing in a pile of clothes, wearing only her pants, and this time she does actually pounce on you.

You wrote a poem about a girl. You don't remember how it went, but it was simple, they always were. Her name was shortened to a letter, and for some reason it made you want her more, it made her intoxicating to you, even though you knew she was your worst enemy. She suffered in the same way you did (mentally defective, broken? Not of the heart, but of the mind) but she made it public, she made it an ordeal, and while you suffered quietly, seeking help, she made it a big deal, she involved others, she made it about her.

You knew you shouldn't but you hated her, you hated what she'd done, you wanted to call her out on it but it wasn't worth it, there was nothing to be gained, only things to be lost. Everyone loved her, no one knew her, they were drip-fed, and because of this they didn't know the truth, they didn't understand what was happening. You tried to make amends, even though you knew you didn't have to, you did it for the sake of peace, for simplicity, you just wanted to be civil, but she wouldn't allow it. The more you tried to make it right, the more she made you out to be in the wrong. Eventually she got engaged, and even though you knew this was it, this was the end of her, you still tried, but still it made it worse, and eventually you let it go, let her walk into her own trapdoor, and she was gone, she was lost, and you let her go, left her to her own devices. In the end, you were better off.

By the time Tuesday starts for you, it's nearly half done for the rest of the time zone. You peel your eyes open, you can't remember the last time they felt like this, you can actually feel how red they are. You grope around for your phone and you're relieved to find it under the pillow, the clock on it telling you it's almost four in the afternoon. You panic, thinking fucking shit what about work? You have a lot of missed calls and texts, and the voicemail notification is present, which is never good. The panic embeds itself. You know you need to do something but not now, now you need water, and Eloise. She's crashed out on the bed next to you, sleeping soundly, so you quietly get up and head for the kitchen. You find a large bottle of Evian in the fridge and drink it all, grabbing another before heading back to the bedroom. Your movements have woken her and she's looking at you as you enter, looking as bad as you imagine you do, as bad as you feel, but in spite of this she's still beautiful, and when she reaches for the water you give it to her, she drinks half, puts it down, and when she does you grab her and try not to let go, you anchor yourself to her, anchor yourself to the world.

You lie like this for a period of time, you're not sure how long it is, but soon you remember about your job, your life, her being rich doesn't give you a free pass to drop your responsibilities. She sees the look of panic on your face and asks you what's up, and you're confused by the look on her face when you simply reply work. She says *Listen to your voicemail,* and you're confused, you tell her you will but first you need to ring work, and she takes your hand and puts it on her left breast, over her heart, and she says *Baby, listen to your voicemail.* You can feel her heartbeat, the smoothness of her skin, the gentle poke of her nipple in your palm, and so you do as she says, somehow her gesture nullifies you, makes her seem right. You only have one voicemail, which is a relief, strange but a relief, and you panic again when you hear your boss's voice, but for some reason she's saying she hopes you're OK, give her a call when you feel up to it, don't worry about the rest of the week and take care of yourself.

Confused, you look over at Eloise, and she has that mischievous look on her face, the one you're growing to love, and you ask her what's up and she says she had a moment of inspiration in a dream and at eight this morning she somehow woke herself up from that dream, rang your boss and said you were in hospital, the diarrhoea was in fact serious food poisoning, you'd be out for the rest of the week at least. You don't know what to say, you don't know how you'll get a sick note, how you'll get away with this, what you're going to do next Monday when you return to work, but these thoughts go away when she takes the phone out of your hand, drops it on the bed and kisses you. Your hand is still on her breast and you squeeze, gently, not sexually, and she kisses you harder and all you do is kiss, for how long you don't know, until you're both tired from the effort, so you stop and just lie there, lie with each other. Eventually you're able to thank her for doing it, and she says it's no problem, any time. The casual way she says this threatens to alarm you but instead it's just tiredness, gratitude, you feel, and you continue to simply lie down.

As much as you don't want to you let her go, only for a moment, and you stretch, the stretch of someone stretching out a lot of sleep, and your head hurts and your nose hurts, you need to blow it but don't want to, not ready to face the redness you know will come out of it. Almost as soon as you let go of Eloise she's phone in hand, tapping away. You hear her groan and you know she's looking at pictures of last night, but you don't want to see them so you don't ask. In spite of this she's uploading them, you just know she is, you wonder why she is, why she'd want this sort of stuff online, when she's just espoused such displeasure at it, but in the same moment you also know, despite it all you had a good time last night, and you know she did, however her good time isn't complete until everyone knows she had a good time.

While she's on her phone you check yours, the missed calls and texts from friends who know you have a girlfriend, who want all the gossip, and while you're sure you'll give it to them in time, you don't want to do it now, so you mark all the messages as read and ignore them. You open Twitter, scroll through, see what's happening in the world. More bad news, little good news, more pointless thoughts from what you consider to be pointless people. It's all so self-indulgent, you think, but then you think this is the twenty-first century, you and everyone else are lying in the bed you have made. You could let it bother you but there's no point, you have Eloise by your side, and that's all you want right now, it makes everything else much less important.

When you put your phone down she's still scrolling, tapping, so you kiss her gently on the arm and say you're going for a bath, come join me when you're ready. You stick your tongue out to make this seem like a joke but in reality you wish she would just put her phone down, spend some time with just you, not you and everyone she knows. The bathroom in the suite is vast, and it takes longer than you need it to to fill the tub. Eventually the water is deep and boiling and you lower yourself in, the water hurting at first, but soon you're used to it and you can almost feel the alcohol and drugs and cigarettes and pain and ache and tiredness being boiled off you. You close your eyes, just for a moment, you hear the door open, she's come into the room, but still your eyes are closed. You only open them when you notice she's not in the tub, not saying anything, and when you can bring yourself to open them you see she's standing over you, phone in hand.

A little while later and you're out of the bath, boiled like a prune but clean, feeling better, she tells you she's deleted the pictures and you tell her you believe her even though you're not sure, but you don't want to challenge her, you don't want to sow seeds of doubt into the relationship. When you had eventually managed to persuade her to put the phone down she got in the bath with you, and she washed you, and you washed her, and you held each other, and while you were holding her you asked her to delete the pictures and she told you she would. Now you're dressed you realise it's been a few days since you exercised, you feel flabby and weak, and you tell her this and she says she hasn't worked out either, she feels the same, do you want to go to the gym? You say of course but you have no clothes, and she says it isn't a problem, you can go shopping, and so now you're in the lift, no key needed this time, and it stops at other floors to let other people in but you both ignore them, holding hands, not talking, in another world, one entirely your own.

You're on the street, the day is nice, but you've been wearing the same clothes for two days now and you don't feel great. You start towards a sports shop you know, generic, chain, cheap clothes for working out in and nothing more, but she doesn't follow, instead mentioning another shop, one you can't afford, and you tell her this in a joking way but with a serious undertone and she says it doesn't matter, and in this moment you know you should be embarrassed, you know you should be trying to discourage her from spending on you, but you also know she's rich, her monthly income from her parents vast, and that it doesn't really matter, if she wants to spend money on you you're going to let her.

So you let her lead you to a store you've never been in, it's fairly large and almost completely empty, a few men in suits, earpieces, one opens the door for you as you approach and greets you and you return the greeting, feeling out of place, but the way she struts around the place you realise you possibly do belong here, after all you belong with her and she's here, so vicariously...

You stand still like a good boyfriend as she picks things off racks and holds them against you, asking you what you think, not really paying attention to your answers, and before long she's shepherding you into a changing room, following you in, the staff don't seem to notice, care, and soon you're stripped down, trying on various pairs of shorts and jogging bottoms and tee shirts and shoes. With each new garment you show her but she's on her phone, only half paying attention, and so you judge for yourself in the full-length mirror, eventually settling on what you think is a gym-appropriate outfit. You know she's been talking while you're sorting yourself out, but you've heard the word like, the word comment, enough to not really be listening, you simply nod, and from the look on her face this is enough to provide the validation she's searching for.

You feel a twinge of guilt as she pays an exorbitant sum for the very little clothing it represents but she takes your hand as you leave the store and squeezes it and this reassures you in a way that means you know it's all OK, it doesn't matter. Back on the street you make your way back to the hotel, the gym being located within it, and she's greeted at the gym as she was at the hotel the previous day, warmly, as if by old friends. You change and put your clothes in a locker, strap the key to your wrist, and you meet her in the gym and just sort of stand there, waiting. You've not been in a gym for a long time, over ten years, and you're lost. You tell her this and she smiles and says it's OK, wait here, and she disappears for a few moments and when she returns she's accompanied by someone in ridiculously good shape, lean, tanned, and muscular, everything you're not and don't want to be but secretly wish you were, and the tee shirt he's wearing bears the name of the gym on it and she introduces you to him, he's one of the personal trainers, he'll help you out.

You tell him about your workout, how it's only new, short, not too strenuous, you've never really been bothered before but in recent weeks, months, you've been drinking too much and you're worried about your figure, you feel like a fool saying so but he tells you it's OK and takes you through some pointers, shows you various machines and how to use them, watches you while you do, and sometime later you're dripping sweat and you hurt all over but it's a good kind of hurt, the kind of hurt you earn, you don't suffer from. She's been by your side this whole time, working out, taking pictures, and you keep wondering why she's taking pictures of you doing certain things, why she'd want to capture these moments, why she'd want to share them, but you know there isn't really a why, it's more of a why not, she has a new boyfriend who's working out and she wants people to see this, telling them isn't enough, will never be enough. By now you've long given up caring what her ex thinks. But what about mutual friends? What about people who know you, are seeing these pictures of you, not sick as you've said, but in the world, living your life? You know you should worry but you can't seem to, you're so wrapped up in Eloise that everything else will surely be fine, will surely take care of itself? She's surely told everyone everything anyway, she probably doesn't even need to post it, but stories don't get likes, they don't get re-grammed and shared, they don't get commented on, at least not in a way that is quantifiable, and so you let her do it, let her share your life online.

By the time you're ready to give it up the trainer is telling you he's impressed, you've done well for a beginner, and you thank him, shake his hand, you don't mind when he wipes his on a towel after, you're both laughing at the awkwardness of it. She's still taking pictures, you wonder if she took any videos, not worrying too much as you haven't said a lot, your voice won't be too evident, this is what you really don't want to hear, and you need a shower and so does she and she says you should do it in the penthouse, not the gym, you can do it together. You grab your clothes from the locker, quickly, and back at the hotel, as the lift ascends, you're excited by the promise of what's to come.

It's early in the evening and you're starving, exhausted by the physical exertions in the gym and the shower, you're not sure when you last ate but you know it wasn't today. You ask her and she concurs, says she's starving too, and that she knows a wonderful restaurant, and you don't even ask, just agree, you're so hungry you're willing to go anywhere. She calls reception and orders a car, not a taxi but a car, and you're excited because you've never been in a car in this way, never had a driver, and you're about to put on your own clothes when she stops you, tells you they won't do, and you feel a little offended but you realise it's OK when she leads you to a closet full of suits, and you want to know why they're here, where they've come from, who they belong to, but you fear the answer so you don't ask the question. You find one that fits, complete with shirt, tie, socks, the whole works, and soon you're dressed and looking in the mirror, making sure it's all OK, and she approaches you, looking incredible in an evening gown, the most beautiful woman you've ever seen in your life, and she tells you you look great, and you believe her.

Her phone goes and she answers, says thanks, tells you the car is here and she takes your arm as you head to the lift, through the reception area, out into the car park, into the back of the car. It's a limo and you can't believe it, you feel out of place, you wonder about the extravagance of it all, but she says why not, she never does this anymore, and you wonder what she means by anymore but you don't pursue it, thinking it might lead to places in her past you're not ready to go to yet. There's a bottle of champagne and you pour two glasses, hand one to her, and you clink them before taking a sip and it tastes expensive, it's nicer than any champagne you've ever had before, you manage half a glass before the limo stops and the driver opens the door and you're outside a restaurant you've seen before, sort of walked past, seen it on the internet and on TV, but you've never really even been too near to it, never even considered going inside.

There's an actual red carpet and you finally get it, you can feel how plush it is even through the shoes you're wearing, and she takes your arm again and there are photographers everywhere and all of a sudden it's just flashes, endless flashes, and you feel blinded and try to stumble into the building but she has a firm grip on your arm, she isn't going anywhere, she's posing, whispering for you to too, but you don't know how to so you stand next to her limply, feeling worthless, wondering why, why all of this, why anything, such a cliché, and after what feels like an age she starts to move and eventually you're inside, the flashing has subsided, you can see again. The maître d' greets her as everyone seems to in this city, like an old friend, the oldest, and they actually hug before he leads her to a table for two, up front, you're not sure but you think this might be the best table in the house, the table small but not too small, dim but not too badly lit. The maître d' seats her and while you seat yourself, he asks about drinks. You're too flummoxed to respond, too overwhelmed by the grandeur of everything, and so you're relieved when she orders another bottle of champagne, you will it to come quickly and you're glad when it does, downing a glass and knowing you look uncouth but not really caring, needing the alcohol in your system to level you out, to numb your nerves.

It doesn't have entirely the desired effect but now you're inside, seated, you feel better, and even though you can feel people looking at you, at the pair of you, at your table, you're mostly able to ignore it, and look at the menu. The prices are beyond anything you've ever imagined from a restaurant, some of the wines cost more than your rent, a lot more, but she looks so at home here and so you try to as well, you want to be part of her world, so you pretend to be confident. She has her phone on the table, you thought being in here might necessitate putting it away but none of the staff seem to mind when she picks it up and taps, does God knows what, you're just glad she doesn't appear to be taking pictures. After a time you order, some sort of pasta dish that better taste good for the cost of it, you think ridiculously as you know you're not paying, and it doesn't take long to come, and you have to admit it is exquisite. After you're both done with your mains you order desserts, sorbet, you've always wondered from reading about it in books and so you can't help yourself, and it's not what you expected but again is amazing, and soon you're full, satisfied, a little buzzed because she keeps ordering champagne, the waiter keeps pouring glasses, you keep drinking them.

Sitting across from her, listening to her talk, looking at her face, being here with her, you know it's probably enhanced by the alcohol but you also know it's true, you know you really like this girl. You haven't felt this way for a long time, maybe only once or twice in total in your entire life, and it wasn't anywhere near this strong, any of those times. Even as she takes selfies in a restaurant that you could only dream of affording to eat in, even as she Facebooks people in what could pass for a ball gown, you realise that these things don't matter, she is who she is and you like her this way. You might even love her this way, but this is definitely too sudden so you don't go down that path, you reel yourself back in to what you know is true, you ignore the speculation, what it might mean.

Soon you're back outside, photographers gone you're pleased to see, and you're back in the car on the way to the penthouse. Even though the photographers didn't accost you outside the restaurant the number of photos taken of you hasn't diminished, she's filled the void, and you're drunk and happy and willing to smile, to pull faces, to wrap your arms around her and let her show the world what you have. Even though it's not for you, it's for her, and though you'll never understand it, you're willing to be a part of it.

There was a time you'd been online, nothing major, just watching things happen, watching the world pass by, checking the news, current events, sports, technology, all the usual stuff, and you'd come across a picture. On Twitter, someone you followed, a court reporter providing details of all the terrible things that happen, making illegality seem like normalcy, and a picture was posted.

It was of people you recognised, former TV presenters, they were outside a courtroom, they took a selfie in which they were smiling, laughing, relaxed, and it upset you because the trial was real, it wasn't trivial, it was serious business but they had tried to reduce it to rubble. The trial was sexual, vulnerable young people being seduced, exploited, used, and if that wasn't enough to make you sad the fact that their plight was belittled really upset you, even if it wasn't their concern you hoped they'd show some respect, they'd at least pretend to care, and the fact that they didn't almost pushed you over the edge. You wondered if it was just you, what it was all about, but ultimately you knew you were in the minority, it wasn't a fight worth taking up, and so you just kept scrolling.

Wednesday brings something you hadn't even considered recently; time apart from her. Even though you initiate it, you want to go home, change clothes, you need to catch up with your parents, it still seems odd, and you're not looking forward to it. The thought of it wrenches you, in a way you hadn't previously thought possible. A wave of feeling washes over you, what would previously be the void replaced by sadness, apathy no more. Which is in itself something of a relief, even if the situation it arises from is anything but. She's disappointed but after a while she understands, she says she's missed too many classes and probably should show her face, and so after a quick room service breakfast you're back in her car, top down, sun out, not a cloud in the sky, cruising towards home.

She drops you off outside your building and you kiss, kiss for a long time, until you're interrupted by a horn and you realise she's blocking the entrance to the car park, so you say bye and get out of the car, watch her pull away, before heading inside. The concierge greets you as he always does, and though sometimes it annoys you for no reason it doesn't today, and you return the hello, feeling generous at greeting him, proud of yourself for doing so. An odd series of events and feelings, quickly forgotten. You check the post, nothing exciting, mostly envelopes for people who no longer live there, pizza flyers, junk, and you press the button for the lift and patiently wait.

Inside your flat you strip all your clothes off, toss them in the basket, collapse naked on the couch, tired even though you slept well, long, deeply. You check your phone, thinking you should return some texts, calls, your Facebook has probably blown up, but you can't face it yet, so you put on some clean clothes and call your mother. She doesn't answer, you forget it's Wednesday and she's busy Wednesday mornings, early afternoons, and so you ring your father instead. He always picks up regardless of what he might be doing, and when he does this time it's good to hear his voice. You catch up, talk about what he's been up to, what you've been up to, and you briefly panic when he questions why you're not at work but you say you are, the lie slipping easily out of your mouth, and you feel bad for it but it's too late, it's out there. The call is good, reassuring, and after you hang up you feel better, no longer tired, ready to face the day.

Reluctantly, wanting to speak to your mother but knowing she still won't be available, you decide to go online instead. You open your laptop, open the browser, head for Facebook first, as so many people do. You're right, it has blown up. Two friends became three once Eloise entered the stage, and now the requests have piled up. You flick through them, people you know, people you don't. People you work with (you think, but maybe not. Do you work anymore?), people you have worked with, faces from another life, another you – pre-Eloise. These last requests are the ones that confuse you, these are people you used to know, haven't spoken to for years, and yet here they are, reaching out, or at least reaching out as much as people care to do these days. You know why it is, it's because you're someone now. You haven't really ever been before, just yourself, son, cousin, nephew, just going through life not letting any fireworks off, not sparking any real interest. But now you're not just you, you're so much more than that; you're half of a couple, and half of a not-just-normal couple? Maybe one day you'll find out if this is true, if rather than normal the couple you're in is special, but for now it doesn't matter. You've been elevated to a position of power, a position that's necessary for others, people will now look up to you, rely on you, and you think it should make you happy but really it's just disinterest you feel, other people's needs have never been your speciality, especially when they're as artificial as this.

Not knowing how to proceed, you don't respond to the requests, you'll deal with them later, instead you check the notifications, knowing what they'll be. You're not wrong, you've been tagged in a million photos, curiosity makes you want to look through them but dread stops you, you've always been an out of sight out of mind person, and you just know that a lot of the photos will be unflattering, will show you at your worst, and so you make sure the notifications are marked as seen and move on. Amongst the tags are God knows how many people liking God knows how many photos of you, people you have never heard of, and comments saying how beautiful Eloise looks, how much of a good couple you make, and these reassure you but not enough to look at them properly, you take the thumbnails, the snapshots of comments, and you move on.

Your Twitter has blown up too, notifications telling of a lot of new followers, and it's the same as before. People you know, don't, used to, and for some reason your ex-girlfriend is in there, you can't help but notice. Your Twitter is open, these aren't requests, and it alarms you and so you scroll through your posts, but there's nothing particularly interesting, nothing outlandish or alarming, mostly semi-drunken rants at one thing or another, nothing new. It's been quiet for the last few days, which proves the pointlessness of it all, the popularity found through inaction, through reputation, through proximity.

You begin to wonder just how many people know Eloise, granted she's rich but not for talent, as far as you know, you still don't know much about her, but merely for luck of birth. You've seen things about her, snippets, but you haven't delved any deeper. If she wants to tell you she will, you're happy to wait. Judging by the number of people suddenly interested in you she must be well known at least, big in certain circles, and as you think about the requests and texts and messages and as your phone goes off again, friends wanting details, wanting to meet for coffees and beers and hang-outs and the like, you wonder how you've never heard of her before. The answer to this doesn't take you long though; gossip columns, magazines, celebrity life, these are things that have never interested you, things you've always actively avoided, not being even a little interested in the lives of others, but now it's too late. Eloise has dragged you into it, and whether you like it or not you're part of it. It all makes sense, and though you wish it didn't you can't avoid it, if it's a part of her it's going to have to be a part of you, and though this thought momentarily saddens you, the sadness is just that, momentary, and you quickly recover. This is who she is, and maybe this explains all the pictures, posts, grams and re-grams and all the rest. She needs you to be a part of it, this is her life and she wants you to be in it. As much as you have tried to avoid it, now you must surrender; now this is your life.

Later on Wednesday and you're lying on the couch, thinking maybe you should eat, ignoring your phone, it keeps ringing, people you don't want to talk to, and you almost stop checking it but the final time you do it's your mother returning your call, and you eagerly pick up. You say hello, so does she, and she sounds happy to hear you and you're always happy to hear her and you talk, catch up, for a long time, talking about your lives, about the family you share, the people you both know, you ask about the cat and the hamster and the garden, it's easy, the conversation flows, it always has, you've always been close. Eventually she says she must go, the phone is pipping as she puts it, her partner is calling, and you say goodbye and tell her you love her and she says the same and hangs up and you're back in the room, back zoning out, and you wonder how to spend your evening.

As if he somehow read your mind, your old flatmate rings, and you pick up, knowing there's no way he could know about Eloise and he doesn't mention it, simply asks what's up? You OK? You up to much tonight? You tell him he read your mind, you have no plans but want some and what's he thinking, and he mentions a film, but you don't fancy the cinema, and then maybe some food, he and his girlfriend are maybe going out, and you say yes and he gives you a time and a place and you tell him you'll meet him there. You do some light exercise, lift some weights, some sit-ups, nothing too strenuous, at heart you're still a lazy person, you always will be, and afterwards you're sweating and tired and you shower, standing under the water, feeling it bring you back to life, make you clean, and you dry yourself and dress and brush your teeth, put on aftershave, feel good about yourself. You think about calling Eloise but you decide not to, you want her to meet your old flatmate but not yet, his girlfriend will go into over-drive and you're not ready, not tonight. Instead you head out alone, meet them in the bar, Belgrave Music Hall, the one you usually go to, if you had a local this would be it, and when you arrive you say your hellos and his girlfriend hugs you and you find it alarming, this has only happened once before and you find it strange, you're not a hug kind of a person, and don't think she is either, but you force yourself not to overthink it, instead you return it briefly before she lets go.

Drinks are ordered and you take them, head up a flight of stairs, two more, and you're on the roof and it's cool without being cold, the sun is up but not out, it's pleasant, and you sit at a table and light a cigarette, and the three of you talk. Apart from seeing her momentarily on Saturday night you haven't seen his girlfriend for a few weeks, which is odd because when you and he lived together you saw her almost every day, and though sometimes it annoyed you mostly it was fine, she's a good person, and so you catch up about the world, your lives, you dodging certain questions, telling certain lies, knowing the truth will reveal itself but not now, not tonight, not in this moment. More drinks are bought and drunk, and soon it's late in the evening and your old flatmate says something about home, maybe soon, but his girlfriend doesn't want to and neither do you, so the idea is dismissed. It's good to be out with them, phones out but not being used, pictures being left untaken, moments that don't need to be captured aren't, and after the last few days it's refreshing and it makes you very happy, the buzz from the alcohol and the real world being observed, it's a good combination.

At some point your phone rings and it's Eloise, and you answer and she says *Hey you* and the way she says it sort of melts your heart, and you say *Hey* back and quietly excuse yourself from the table, still not wanting her to be known yet, to them anyway, savouring the break from that new part of your life. But the break is short-lived as she asks what you're up to, and you tell her, and she says *Cool, I love it there*, and you immediately have your back to the wall but you don't mind, not really, and you invite her and she agrees and says she'll be there soon. You get back to the table and your flatmate's girlfriend says *Who was that?* And even though it's a question you don't think should be asked, you say that was Eloise, and immediately she's all over it: *Who's Eloise? Eh? Eh?* And so you tell her, *Eloise is my girlfriend*, and she almost

shrieks because she's wanted this for so long, you've always sus-
pected she wants to double-date, but even with this she's a good
person and wants you to be happy. She asks what Eloise is like
and you say you can see for yourself, she's on her way here now.

It isn't long before she arrives, and she immediately ingratiates
herself into the group by arriving with a tray of drinks, you'd
texted her the order, and it's smiles and handshakes and intro-
ductions all round. Straight away it's the third degree, she's being
quizzed by your flatmate's girlfriend, while your old flatmate just
looks at you with a knowing look, he's impressed, and you're
happy he is because you like him, you like his approval, and
any previous thoughts of home are definitely banished, more and
more drinks are bought and drunk and Eloise is buying them
all, buying friendship, which is crass but it's working, and you
don't mind, you're too drunk to feel bad about not spending any
money, and she's taking pictures, asking strangers for group shots,
and even though you and your old flatmate are uncomfortable,
not entirely but fairly, you both let it happen, both with women
to please, both with happiness now dependent on factors out of
your control, both with other people to worry about, because
by now his girlfriend is into it, and even though she hasn't said
anything you think she recognises Eloise, knows who she is, and
you're sure these pictures will be uploaded twice, on two Facebooks and Instagrams, but you're drunk and you don't care and
the time flies and soon it's the early hours, your old flatmate
and his girlfriend both have work in the morning, and you say
you do too, which is technically true, even if you're not actually
going, and Eloise says she has class and you say your goodbyes
and Eloise comes back to yours and you fool around but it's late,
you're both tired and drunk, so you do no more than fool around
before you put your arms around her and let sleep take you.

There had been a wedding, it was a Saturday, in June, the first
week of summer, a heatwave, and each part of the day, each
chapter of the book of marriage, had taken place in one room,
which meant between chapters, when doors were opened and

furniture moved, you were shepherded outside. It wasn't a bad thing, it was warm and sunny and there was a bar, so you were content.

You were with a friend you hadn't seen for years, literally, you didn't know how many, and you were meeting his girlfriend for the first time and she was nice, great, just like him really, which was a good thing because he was a good person. You'd always harboured a little hatred for him but it was born from jealousy, and you never let it show, it wouldn't have been fair, it wasn't his fault.

You had been the only single person at the wedding. The number of guests had been uneven, each table set for eight except yours, which was for nine. You'd spent the week building up to it dreading it, the morning of it you almost didn't go, but you had to go, you couldn't not. And so with a sense of apprehension so big it almost broke you, you went. And you had a great time. It had turned out to be a really good day. You'd seen old friends, met new friends, watched a very good friend get married. You'd drunk, danced, been in a good mood all day. You'd gone home happy. And you'd woken up the following day as the loneliest man on the planet.

Thursday dawns bright, you forgot to close the blinds last night, you are back to your old self again. That didn't take long. The light hurts your eyes and you roll over, wanting more sleep, but you feel a poke, she's already awake, and now you are too she wants you to stay awake. Without opening your eyes you roll over to her, drape your arm across her chest, not with any real purpose, mostly just to make the connection you know she wants. Your eyes do soon open however, at the sound of the familiar click as she takes a picture of you. As you always do, you let it slide, she needs these pictures to happen more than you need them not to, so you take them in your stride, every last one. You kiss her to make her stop, but it doesn't work, she kisses you back but doesn't let go of her phone, she clicks and clicks as you kiss and kiss, it's a war, one that she wins, because soon you stop kissing, but she's still taking pictures.

What are we doing today? you ask her. *I don't know what you're doing*, she replies, *but I have to go to school.* At least that explains why she's awake so early, you think to yourself, and the thought reassures you, you could do with a lie-in. You ask her what time it is and she says eight, she's going in the shower because she has to be in for nine, needs to stop for some food on the way. She kisses you softly before getting up, and you can't help but watch her walk away, she's only wearing one of your tee shirts, and it makes you feel safe, your marker is on her, and even though you know she's yours emotionally, it's good to have physical reassurance. You roll back over, closing your eyes, and before you know it she's shaking you awake, saying she has to go. You tell her you don't want her to, even though you know she has to, and she reiterates this point, which you accept, and a kiss later she's out of the door. You let sleep take you again, welcoming its embrace.

By the time you wake again it's nearly midday, you're refreshed, and so you get up, drink some juice from the fridge and begin your workout. It's only the second week you've been doing it, so it's still fairly timid, but it's enough to work up a sweat, and when you weigh yourself in the bathroom you see it's working, you've lost some weight. Not a lot, but enough to let you know it's not all for nothing, and you're very pleased to know this. After a quick shower and a breakfast that's actually probably brunch of some leftover salad you find in the fridge, your phone vibrates and it's a text from your old flatmate, all it says is nice. You message back I know right? And then commences a rare but occasional manly conversation, the kind you don't often participate in, but feel you have to have every once in a while, so as not to disappoint your sex. You know he's not going to tell anyone so you tell him it's going really well, she's so hot and her body is so tight, and you almost feel bad but you don't, not really, it's nice to be able to brag for once. He asks you how work is and you avoid the question, feeling a pang of guilt, but the guilt soon goes away when she messages you, just saying hey. It's all she needs to say, you're probably wrapped around her little finger based on the speed of your reply but you don't mind, of all the fingers in the world you could be wrapped around you're glad it's this one, and you say hey back and the next message is a picture, it's her, she's naked, and it immediately turns you on until you notice she's not alone, she's in a studio, and your mind starts racing as you wonder what the hell is going on.

You decide to be indirect, hoping she'll volunteer information as to what's going on, and you ask her how school is. She tells you it's a total drag, her classes were pointless but she had to at least show up, and now she's modelling, part of the mark for the course is taking part in extra-curricular activities, and she chose life modelling for hers. This is the explanation, not the one you wanted, but it makes sense anyway. You must take too long with your reply, because before you can write and send it she messages you again, saying she hopes it's OK, it's only art, it's not sexual, and you tell her you know and that it's fine, even though you don't really think it is, you're not really happy with it, but you don't tell her this, you couldn't even if you wanted to, it's not really your place, and besides it would most likely start an argument that you can't, won't win, she's right, it is OK really, even if you don't like it. She tells you it isn't often, once or twice every few months, and this reassures you, but only slightly, you're still decidedly uncomfortable, and you know you're going to carry this discomfort with you no matter what she says, so you tell her honestly it's fine, and you feel bad for lying but isn't that what it's all about? If life were all honesty everyone would hate each other, and you definitely do not want her to hate you, so you reassure her, you play the part of the good boyfriend, and soon she's relieved and tells you she has to go, it's time to keep still, but she won't be long and then she's coming over, she has something important to tell you.

You say bye and put your phone down, then feel your heart hit the floor. She has something important to tell you? You're sure it can't be bad, you rack your brain looking for possible clues, anything she could have said or done to lead to this, anything you could have said or done to make her say this, and you're panicking, you always do, you're going through all the worst possible scenarios in your head and your imagination is running wild. You need a drink. There's nothing in the flat so you head downstairs to the shop, pondering over the beer and wine aisle before realising this won't do, you head to the counter and get a bottle of rum and a bottle of gin. Rum to make you feel better, to settle you, gin when rum gets too sweet, for when you inevitably need to prolong the drunk but your mouth is sticky and the thought of more rum isn't a pleasant one. You pick up some tonic for the gin, nothing for the rum, and soon you're back in your flat, on the couch, glass of ice and rum in hand, sipping it slowly, enjoying the taste, resenting what it represents.

You need some reassurance, so you ring your friend, the one dying for all the gossip, and even though she's at school, should be teaching, she answers almost immediately. She doesn't even say hello, she simply tells you to tell her all, and before you know it you are, you're telling her every minute detail, and she's so happy for you until you tell her what Eloise said, something important, and she's now worried for you, she's telling you she's sure it's fine, it's probably nothing, and you want to believe her but you can hear the doubt in her voice, she sounds sympathetic already, and this only serves to make you feel worse, and as the sips of the rum get bigger you realise it's not working, calling your friend, afternoon drinking, it's all making everything worse, so you decide to head out, into town, you need to distract yourself, not dwell on yourself, and so you get up, swaying under the effect of the alcohol, and head out the door.

The streets feel different, brighter and duller at the same time, things seem much better, but they also seem much worse, everything is put into perspective, but not one that you can grasp. You light a cigarette as you walk, focusing on it to distract yourself from what is to come, from what might be, and even though you think it could be fine, you try to tell yourself it could all be OK, you don't believe yourself, you're just not that guy, you're a pessimist through and through, and so you smoke, you ignore the truth, you just keep walking. There are people everywhere, normal people, going about their lives, and you're jealous of them, they look so happy, they seem so content, and even though you know they probably have issues just like you do, you ignore that fact, you allow their apparent happiness to bleed into you, to affect you, you juxtapose their joy against your sorrow and wallow in the feeling.

You take a swig from the hip flask you don't remember filling up, bringing with you. It was a sort of present from your old flatmate before he moved out, and you've filled it with rum, you allow the warmth to spread through you, it softens everything, it makes things feel like they might be OK, you can't freak out in public, not here, not with all these people around to see, and you're reassured by this fact. You check your phone, for once it's silent, and though this would normally be a good thing right now it unnerves you, the longer it's silent, the longer she's naked in front of strangers, the longer you're kept in doubt. You want to tell her how you really feel, you wish you could tell her that it should only be you, no one else should see her the way you do, but you can't, it wouldn't be fair, and so you have to accept it, you have to carry on.

You put your headphones in, you're glad you brought them, because even though the music doesn't reassure you, if anything it makes you feel worse, it's at least happening, it's something you can hold on to, the lyrics let you know that you're not alone, that other people feel this way, the situations may not be the same but the emotions are, it's all shared, it's all distracting. You want to text her, you want to tell her how you feel, but you can't, it's not that simple, it should be but it isn't, and so you keep walking. You walk, and walk, and when you focus on the walking it almost makes you feel better, it almost makes everything OK. A lyric you hear makes you want to scream, and the words seem as if they're screaming to you, directly at you, but they're not, you're not the only one hearing them, they're not for you, they're for someone else, they just... are. You wish you weren't so sad, but it's a wish you've wished a million times before, and it never gets answered, never once has that wish come true, and so you keep walking.

You take a selfie, it's not something you'd ever normally do, but it makes you feel closer to her, it's what she'd do, and you take it and send it to her, you hope she'll understand, and when she replies with a simple smiley face you know it's lost, the meaning is only for you, the point is lost, you want to tell her what it is, but you know it's pointless. And so you keep walking, you walk up streets, down streets, you cross roads, you just walk. Before long you end up at your favourite bar, and you enter, it's quiet, but it doesn't matter, just being inside almost makes things better, just the sight of other people makes you feel like it could be OK.

You order a beer, you take a seat, you sip the beer and stare at your phone as if it holds some kind of meaning, some sort of answer, and though it could, it doesn't right now. You sip your beer, look at your phone, sip, phone, this goes on until the glass is empty, and you order another, repeat the process. Soon you're more drunk than you should be this early in the afternoon, and this alone, but as long as you know she's waiting for you, waiting to say something important, something deadly, you can't help yourself, and you're talking to the girl behind the bar, flirting, and you hate yourself for it but you can't stop yourself, you feel like you need a plan B, you feel like you need to get one up on her, if she's going to dump you it doesn't matter, because this girl behind the bar likes you. You're so fucking stupid it's unbelievable, and you know it, but you do it anyway.

Eventually your phone rings and it's her, she's coming to yours, and you're not sure if you should say you're not there, you want to tell her you're at the bar, but you don't want her to make assumptions, you don't want to reveal your fear, and so you sit in limbo, wondering, wishing you had any idea what to do.

By the time you finish your current beer you realise that hiding isn't the answer, you have to face her, and so you pay the tab and leave the bar, light a cigarette, smoking it as if it might be your last. You walk home, slower than you normally would, but with a purpose, if you're going to get dumped, you're going to pretend it's all OK, and so you walk, trying not to drag your feet, and soon you're outside your building, and there's no sign of her so you let yourself in, you get in the lift, you ascend the floors full of trepidation, full of fear, full of thoughts of what might come next. You take a selfie, send it to her, almost as a peace offering, you want her to know you're the same, you're just like her, the selfie is an olive branch, you want it to show her that you can be what she wants, you want to be everything to her, and even though there's no signal in the lift, it comes back unsent, you ignore it, you pretend it sent, you pretend she understands, you try not to weep.

The lift hits floor twenty-six and you step out, and you're thrown when she's outside your door, she's waiting for you, and she looks confused, she thinks you're inside, and she asks where you've been and you avoid the question, you take her hand, worried it might be the last time. You open the front door, you let her walk in, you're trying your hardest but you can't stop your legs from shaking, your whole body soon joining in. You ask her if she wants a drink and she says *No, maybe, she doesn't know, soon*, she has to tell you something. Her indecisiveness does nothing to reassure you, so you focus on other things, something concrete, something that isn't her. As you close the front door you look into the hall, you look for a saviour but there isn't one to be found. She sits on the couch, and you stand next to her, and she says *Please sit down, I really have to tell you this*.

She must be able to see the fear in your eyes, because she takes your hand, smiling, she tells you it's OK, you have nothing to worry about, but you're worried anyway, you can't help but be, and so what she says next is even more of a shock to you than you knew it would be, it's even bigger than you expected, you can't process the information, you just sit and look at her. You know you're expected to say something but you have no words, you're too taken aback, and soon the silence becomes a cloud, it's hovering over the pair of you, it's taken on natural characteristics, and it's alarming to you both.

Her words: *I love you*.

The words you're supposed to want to hear, all through your entire life you've been told this is all that matters, events happen, people come and go, you can be rich or poor, happy or unhappy, popular or ignored, you can be anything, but unless someone is saying these words to you your life is meaningless, you as a person are worthless. The words hang there, and when you're eventually able to understand them, to grasp their meaning, you start to smile, beaming at her, it's only been a few days but you feel the same, and so you say *I love you too*. She begins to smile, then beams back at you, and soon you're sitting, beaming at each other like a pair of idiots, neither of you sure of how to proceed, and so you pull her towards you and kiss her, then hold her, hold her close and hold her tight, you lie back on the couch and pull her on top of you and hold her in place, hold her like the rock she has become, your rock. Soon she's kissing you and you're kissing back and you know this is going to be the first time since you've exchanged those words and it's more magical, somehow, it means more, it's more intense, more physical, it doesn't last long but it doesn't need to, right there on the couch you're both spent, satisfied.

After you've both re-dressed she asks if you're drunk and you say *No, not anymore. I might be a little drunk on you though.* And it's a cliché and you hate yourself for saying it but she likes it, and you excuse yourself to go to the toilet and as you return to the room your phone vibrates, a text from your friend saying *Oh my God, congratulations*, and you wonder how she knows, but you can see Eloise on her phone, and this is all the clue you need, so you open Facebook and yes, there it is, Eloise has told the world what you've told her. You're not annoyed, not really, even though you think it's personal, it's something between the pair of you that doesn't involve anyone else – you don't mind her sharing, you do sort of understand now what people mean when they say they want to shout from the top of the mountain, it all suddenly makes sense. She says you should go out and celebrate, and you agree, she mentions a champagne bar, one that's too pricey for you, but you know she's going to pay anyway. This is what she does, it's her way of making herself feel connected, one of many ways, and though it's not something you completely understand you know that she needs it and so you let it happen. And you're trying to put your shoes on but she's taking pictures, she wants to capture this moment and for once you're completely responsive, completely open to the idea, you think this is a moment that does need capturing.

You smile, laugh, you're happy, genuinely happy, and for a second you remember how you felt earlier, the fear, the anticipation, and you laugh at yourself, thinking what a fool you'd been. And you reflect – genuine happiness. When was the last time you felt this? You begin to wonder but quickly stop yourself – that's a thread that doesn't need pulling. The lid needs to stay firmly on that can of worms. Stop thinking about the past and for once in your life enjoy the present. Try anyway.

She finally lets you put your shoes on in peace, and after you have, and she's put hers on you take her in your arms, you hold her, and you whisper in her ear *I love you*, and she whispers *I love you*, and you know this is how it's going to be, these words are going to frame all that happens from now on, but this is not a bad thing, life is always going to be framed, you just have to make sure it's a good frame, one that you can enjoy, one that will support you, and as you release her from your grasp, sliding your hands down her arms until your hands are in hers, you look at her, Eloise Dunhill, this woman, your woman, and in this moment you feel like one person, you feel like you are inside of her, and you know she's inside of you, and you don't say anything, you just look at each other, and eventually the moment passes and you're out the door.

She says something about a taxi but it's late afternoon, sunny, and you're in such a good mood you don't think you can sit still so you tell her you want to walk and she says OK, and you're holding hands, walking down the familiar streets, which for the second time today feel different, but this time they are definitely brighter, there's no mistaking it, the people seem even happier, there are birds in the sky, a sky containing no clouds. You pass a person walking a dog and Eloise briefly pets it, and you do too, your hatred for dogs washed away in a sea of love, and you wonder how it got this good, what you've done to deserve to feel like this, you've wondered this so many times before but never in a good way, and it's refreshing, your entire life has turned upside down but in a good way, and you're just so happy.

After the dog and its walker have been allowed on their way Eloise is on her phone. You playfully ask her who she's texting, anyone interesting, and she says not really, she's just telling everyone that you love her, and you love this about her, you love that she's proud of your love, you realise she probably wants you to tell people but you're not going to, not yet – you plan to tell your mum, your dad, but that can happen tomorrow. Right now it's all Eloise, she's all you have and all you want. You pass a church, not even able to muster a look of disdain because of how good you feel, you smile as she takes a selfie of you both, you laugh when she sends it to you, too happy to even bother about how you look, you just look at her, her face, how well defined it is, how her eyes focus in on you, bore into you; you feel like she can see into your soul and you don't mind because it belongs to her now, all that you are and ever will be belongs to her.

Eventually you're at the bar, Epernay; you've been in before but only once, with a friend you don't know anymore, and you can see her checking in online, she's still showing off, and though this would have annoyed you before, earlier this week – it still would if anyone else did it – you're becoming more and more immune to it, you notice it less and less, it's becoming part of your life and there's nothing you can do about it, just accept it. You know she has to have her life online as well as in the flesh, and so while she does you order the most expensive bottle of champagne (this is how you order it, feeling like an idiot but not caring) and the bartender asks if you're celebrating and you say *Yes, it's a great day*, and you know he wants to ask but knows it's not his place so you give him the information he wants. You say to him *We're celebrating life, love. We're celebrating us.*

One bottle of champagne turns into two and then the growth seems exponential, soon it's late and you're drunker than you planned to be and you think almost everyone in the bar has taken a picture of the two of you, including the bartender, and they're all happy to oblige because Eloise has bought them all a bottle of champagne – you dread to think how many the bar has gone through – and soon you're stumbling out the door, heading to a club, Wire, that's just about near enough to drag yourselves to, and though you've never been a fan, despite its sharing a name with one of your favourite songs, it's the only half-decent place to go on a Thursday night. The bouncer doesn't really want to let you in, but after Eloise slips him a note he's happy to open the door for you; he actually has to escort you down the stairs – yes it's that kind of club, literally underground – and the music is loud, the room is dark, packed with bodies, they're all moving as one, moving their bodies to the music.

You go to the bar and get a beer each, not really wanting them but needing to prolong the drunk, needing to have something to do with at least one of your hands, and you occasionally sip from it, not really tasting it, having already drunk enough and smoked enough that nothing really has a taste, not anymore. Eloise disappears to what you assume is the toilet; she said something to you but the music is so loud you can't hear anything, you just nodded and watched her walk away. She's soon back, and she looks wired, and you think you know why and your suspicions are confirmed when she slips you a small baggie and ushers you to the toilet yourself. You slip into a cubicle and do a couple of keys, but the coke isn't great, it's cut too much, and though you know you'll regret it in the morning you keep doing it anyway, needing to offset the drunk, and even though it's bad coke you do enough that it hits anyway, and soon you're wired, and when you realise that you're wired inside Wire you spend too long laughing at the fact, before eventually composing yourself and exiting the cubicle. You check yourself in the mirror, dust off the coke moustache you've created, and head back into the room.

Eloise is waiting outside the toilet and she takes your hand, drags you to the dance floor, and the pair of you join the moving bodies, you become part of the crowd, and everyone seems to have their eyes closed, they look serene yet intense at the same time, they look relaxed but if you look closely enough you can see how hard they're all trying, you can see they just want to fit in. Closed eyes suit you, you know how wired you look, and you look at Eloise and her eyes are closed, and so you close yours too, you move without caring, motion without regard, you let the music take you, let your heartbeat match the beat of the music, you try to match your body to the rhythm and even though you're sure it doesn't you don't care, can't care, not right now.

When you eventually open your eyes a minute, an hour, later, Eloise is talking to some people you don't know, don't recognise, you think you've never seen them before, and as always her phone is out, she's taking pictures, they're taking pictures, and before long she drags you in to them and the people you don't know have their arms around you, and you feel their sweat, and it should disgust you but it doesn't, it's so hot in the place that there is sweat in the air, it's all around you, it's part of who you are in this moment. After what seems like a lifetime, probably a million pictures, Eloise's friends move on, she slips her phone back into her purse, you dread to think how you'll look in the pictures, who'll look at them, but that's tomorrow's concern, that's for future you to deal with, and so you let her put her arms around your neck, you put yours around her waist, you can't help but touch her behind, it feels good, everything does right now, except your nose but that's the sacrifice you make, and you're full of energy, pumped, and you just keep dancing.

The club has a photographer and Eloise insists, you let her, and before you know it people are joining you in the photo, strangers forcing their way into your life, and soon you're not even in the picture. People in here seem to recognise Eloise and they want pictures with her, she's given drinks, she puts her arm around people, she smiles and poses and she looks good, you have to admit to yourself, and you want a cigarette but since the stupid law came into force you know you'll have to wait, you're not willing to get kicked out of the club, possibly fined, just for a cigarette and so you start to dance, on your own, but it doesn't matter, no one cares, you don't care, you're too wired to care about anything. When Eloise finally drags herself away from the people, the strangers, you drag her up the stairs, it's easier going up than coming down, you both abandoned your beers a long time ago, mostly undrunk, unwanted, and once you're outside the fresh air is good, it feels good on your sweaty skin, you're cold but it's refreshing, and your hands are shaking as you light your cigarette but eventually it takes, the smoke feels good in your lungs, it's reassuring, it reminds you of things you didn't know about, weren't sure of.

She has her phone out again and she's talking into it, shouting, and it's past midnight but from the sounds of it the other person doesn't mind, you wonder if they're rich too, if they're nocturnal like you imagine most young, rich, beautiful people to be, and Eloise is telling the person on the other end of the phone where she is, what's happening, and she says that's a great idea! And hangs up, then you can see she's uploading photos, then she's checking likes, comments, she's telling a wider audience about her life, and you reluctantly pull your phone out of your pocket but all you do is check the time, read old messages, put it away, you're not that interested in the virtual world, you have enough problems with the real one. At least you used to, it doesn't seem like you do anymore, everything seems OK. Back in the club and a couple of bumps later and you're sitting down, in a corner booth, people are crowding in with you, and the night will go like this; you'll try to listen, you won't hear anything, so you'll mirror other people's expressions, laughing when they do, looking serious when they do, and you don't know these people, you don't want to be in their pictures, you don't want to be part of their lives, but under the table Eloise is holding your hand and because of this you tolerate everything else, in reality you know everything is going to be OK.

You're not sure when Thursday ended, when Friday began, because you don't make it to bed; instead once the club kicks you out, you find another club that's open until the early hours, one that you've never been to before, you don't even catch the name of it, you simply let her pull you into it, you let her feed you drugs and make you dance and you know you should be tired but you're not, you're wired, and more photos are taken, you manage a few sips of a few drinks, it's all a blur really, but as long as she's by your side that's all that matters, she's in focus, you don't care that nothing else is. It's only when your nose starts to bleed, and you can't seem to get it to stop, that you decide to call it a night, you take her hand and lead her outside, into the cold light of day.

You check your phone and it's nearly eight in the morning, your colleagues will all be on their way to work, already there, and you've not even managed to go to bed, you don't remember when you last ate but you're not hungry, your mouth is dry but you're not thirsty, your body aches but you're not tired. You ask her what she wants to do and she says back to yours, chill out, go from there, and you've not had a bump for a while because of your nose, so by the time you get home the effects have mostly worn off, and you're glad to sit down, you're glad there's no music and you're no longer dancing. She's taking pictures, actually you think she might be filming something, the view, herself, and she's talking into the camera on her phone, it seems like a video diary, and when she points it at you you cover your face, this isn't your kind of thing even at the best of times, let alone after having been awake all night, and you're covered in blood. You tell her you're going in the shower, and once you're in there it's too much effort to stand, you sit and let the water wash over you, and you have no energy, it's all been spent, and it takes an age to stand up, wash, dry off and join her on the couch.

From nowhere she's got some weed and you share a joint, it's the mellow kind of high you've missed, you prefer it to the coke high, and the towel slips off but you don't mind, you're immediately very stoned, the lack of sleep and food and the alcohol and other drugs still in your system means you're vulnerable, you know you must look stupid sitting there naked while she's fully dressed, but it's 9am on a Friday morning and you just don't care. It's not long before she goes in the shower and while she's in you check your phone, no texts or calls, which is good because you're not sure you can face human interaction right now. You go online, lots of crap on Facebook, more friend requests, more picture tags, more comments, more things to ignore, and you go on Twitter and there's more followers, more tweets, and you ignore these too, you're not fooled by this sudden popularity, you know it has nothing to do with you, it's entirely two-dimensional. You're curious about the pictures of you from last night but they probably won't be uploaded yet, which is good because you're not ready to look. Bored, you go to Google, search Eloise Dunhill, see what else might come up that you haven't seen on her social media. You wonder why this hadn't crossed your mind before, but quickly dismiss the thought. If you spent too much time wondering about all the things you had and hadn't done, you'd be bound to lose your mind. What little remained anyway.

You realise you must be out of touch when there's a lot about her, articles, photos, links to her social media pages, she seems to be more famous than you'd previously anticipated, not exactly A-list but not unheard of. She clearly has a lot of famous friends, still not A-list but closer than her, and these seem to have elevated her status. Elevated her to a status at which you should have heard of her. You should have at least known her name. You should have, for once, not been such a fucking idiot. You read a few articles, but it's nothing interesting, the usual gossip nonsense, she bought some clothes one time, another time she drank a coffee, she once, shock horror, went to a restaurant. It's all superficial rubbish so you disregard it, think about calling your mother, telling her about Eloise, you want Eloise to meet her, and when you realise this you smile, because you know it's big. You're close to your mother, and you want Eloise to be too. You guess that subconsciously it's probably something to do with seeking approval but that's incidental, you might end up spending your entire life with Eloise, your mother will have to meet her eventually, why not now? Plus, you wonder if Eloise would like to see the village your mother lives in, it's out of the way, there won't be people taking pictures there, and on top of this you want to her see where you grew up, you want to take her to certain spots in the town you grew up in, show her parts of the city, which in turn become parts of yourself. When she comes out of the shower you ask if she wants to and she's delighted, even more so than you'd thought she might be, and she's saying when? *When can we go? Why not this weekend?* And you think why not, no time like the present, and so while Eloise dries her hair, gets dressed, texts and WhatsApps and Facebooks you ring your mother.

You realise what time it is too late but she picks up anyway, you didn't expect her to, she might be having breakfast or still be in bed, but anyway she answers and you say hello, happy to hear her voice, and she returns the greeting and sounds concerned, which you understand, you only spoke a few days ago, normally you speak every week or two so two calls in less than one week is cause for concern, she knows your past, she worries. You tell her it's OK, nothing to worry about, in fact quite the opposite, and you ask her what she's doing this weekend, and by that you mean will she be at her partner's, or will her partner be at hers? She says her partner will be at hers and you say good, you're going to come and see them, you have a surprise. She asks what it is but you say that would ruin the surprise, you mention a pub, one that does exceptional food, and ask her to book a table for four. You're grinning while you say this, and she immediately picks up on the fact you've said four, she mentions the name of a friend, asks if she's back in the country, and you say *No, she's still abroad, but I'm going to bring my girlfriend.* Your mother sounds delighted, and the conversation ends with you saying you'll tell her all tomorrow, her saying she'll make the booking.

When you turn back to Eloise she's looking at you, beaming, phone in hand, and you ask if she's OK and she says it's really nice to hear you say it, girlfriend, so you say it again, *You are my girlfriend,* and she almost explodes. You ask if she was taking pictures of you on the phone with your mother, and she says of course, it's sweet, and you ask if they're going to be online and she says they already are and you sigh, but it's not a big sigh. It's not a big deal. It especially doesn't matter when she kisses you, and you kiss her back and soon you're in bed and you think, everything that exists is already on the internet, what damage can a little more do?

There was a time you were at university, a night of drinking, which was the norm, a night of drinking alone, which wasn't the norm but was far more frequent than it should have been. You'd drunk so much you were in bed by half past ten, no desire for more music or films and you couldn't face watching any more of *The Simpsons* on DVD, so you'd rung your girlfriend. She was a few years younger than you, still in your home town, and you spoke every day, not because you wanted to, but because she insisted, the relationship was good but she was possessive, obsessed, and though you liked her you never had much to say, and besides you'd always hated talking on the phone.

So you'd rung her, and talked for the requisite amount of time, she knew you were drunk, she always did, you weren't subtle, and eventually you'd run out of things to say, so you'd started singing. You'd sung 'Tiger Lily', a song that didn't mean any- thing between the two of you but which you liked regardless, and you'd sung it in full to her, and half-way through she'd started to cry. You couldn't possibly figure out why, you were drunk and slurring and you had an awful singing voice, out of tune and monotonous, but you'd sung anyway, she'd cried any- way, and you never asked why and soon after you'd finished the entire song you'd hung up, fallen asleep, barely remembered the episode the following morning.

She'd never asked why you'd sung, and you'd never asked why she'd cried, and it had never happened again.

You decide to drive across your original home city on Friday night, the delight that is Hull, and so now you're in her car, she's driving the motorway, eating up the miles, and you're scared and excited at the same time. You've booked a hotel, you wanted to go middle of the road but she insisted, and so on her credit card you've booked the biggest suite in the biggest hotel, dead in the centre. You've never stayed in a hotel in this city and you're kind of excited, you're excited for her to see the place too, but you're also nervous, it isn't the best city in the world, you can't imagine how it'll look without the rose-tinted glasses on. And so you're quiet in the car, she is too but the silence isn't uncomfortable, it's completely the opposite, and in this moment you feel very much that you're in the right place, not physically but emotionally, metaphysically, everything is going so right and while you can't understand it you don't try to, you don't want to second-guess your own happiness so you accept it, embrace it, you let it become you.

The drive doesn't take long, less than an hour on quieter motorways, they always are heading into the city this time on a Friday, at this time everyone else is heading out, which is understandable, there isn't a great deal going on really to stick around for. You check in at the hotel and you're alarmed to see someone you recognise, someone you went to school with working in the place, but they don't see you, or if they do they don't recognise you, and you see a few people nudge each other and less than subtly point at Eloise, but she doesn't see, and you don't bring it up, it's becoming a more frequent occurrence, or maybe it isn't and you're just noticing it more, and there's no point getting hung up on it, in a bad or a good way, and so once her credit card is handed over and keys given in return you ascend to the suite, it's only a few floors up, and when you open the doors you can see the disappointment written on her face, but only for a second, she quickly dismisses it and smiles at you, telling you it looks nice. You love her for pretending, and you kiss her, gently, and you had planned to unpack but instead you fall into bed, into her, into love all over again, and though it doesn't take long neither of you mind, and after holding each other in bed, lying with each other not saying anything, just accepting each other's presence, she showers, and after she's done you shower too, and once you're both dressed and ready you head out into the city.

You walk slowly, hand in hand, you're pointing things out to her, and in your suit trousers and shirt you feel like an upmarket tour guide, and you like it, you're enjoying it, and she seems to be too, her attention is unwavering, she doesn't interrupt, she asks the right questions at the right times. When you're standing outside the hotel you point to the bus station, and the shopping centre, and say *These weren't here when I was a kid, they're not that old, it's part of the regeneration of the city*, and she insists on taking your picture at every turn, you end up with one outside each landmark you point out, and you love her for these pictures, you know these buildings mean nothing to her but she knows they do to you, and her capturing them makes you feel needed, it makes your past feel important, and you let her take a million pictures, upload them all, you let her tag you outside places, you let her tell the world.

You pass a bar near the train station you used to drink in waiting for trains, the bank you used to work in, the fast food place you also used to work in, and you know she can't imagine these things. She can picture you in them, working hard, earning your money, but it's not part of her world, she's never had a job, and you can't imagine this, but you can picture each other's lives, appreciate each other's journeys, you're just glad they caused your paths to cross. You take her inside the shopping centre, which has always been there, but is much changed nonetheless. You stop at the bottom of the escalator to the cinema, not going up, simply saying *This wasn't a cinema when I was younger*. It was shops, and there was a café you spent your weekends with friends, it was the only place you could smoke inside that wasn't a pub you were too young to get into then, and you'd get fizzy drinks and chips and just sit and talk and smoke, for hours on end, for a long time, good memories with what were good friends.

You walk down the next street, point out the shop where you used to spend all your wages as a teenager, telling her about all the CDs you used to buy, you tell her you still have them all in a box somewhere, you're not sure where, and she tells you she wants to see them and you promise her she can. You pass bars you started to drink in as you grew older, your ID letting you in, all the bars are faceless, you don't know their names, you never did, you just remember vague nights being in them, drinking the time away, spending time with friends, making memories, growing up. You pass the tattoo parlour where you had yours done, and you stand outside for a long time, peering into the dark shop, the church at your back looming ominously over you and she asks about it but there's nothing you can say, you've never been inside, it was never a part of your life. You pass the restaurant you plan to take her to because there's one last place you want to show her: the marina. You sit on a bench on the edge of the river, and you tell her this is where you spent your early teenage years, just you, your friends and some skateboards, too many weekends to count just skating up and down this marina, trying to learn new things, your friends succeeding, you failing but not caring, trying anyway. You tell her this is where it all began, this is probably where you started the path to who you are now as an adult, and though there are other factors, other events that hold more significance, you're not ready to tell her these yet, these can come later.

You sit side by side, your arm around her shoulders, her head resting on yours, and you don't say anything, just look out onto the water, watch the lights of the buoys flash on and off, warning boats, you point out the bridge to her, tell her you'll take her to it tomorrow, there are things there you want her to see, and you feel her snuggle in to you and she's warm, soft, she feels alive, and it makes you feel alive and she's not taking any pictures and you ask her why and she says *I don't need to, not right now, this is just for us*, and this makes you want to cry and though she ruins the moment by then taking a few anyway it doesn't matter, you know that for a moment this place belonged to you, and you tell her you love her, you'll always love her, and really nothing else matters you think, nothing else ever will, this is all there will ever be.

You arrive at the restaurant, it's only a chain Italian place but you've never been in, always wanted to, and besides two people you used to know work here, two of the few people from your past you actually try to stay in contact with, and you're not surprised to learn the place is fully booked, but you are surprised when all of a sudden there is a table, you hadn't even given your names and the maître d' is saying *Please follow me Miss Dunhill*, and then you know what's happening, you know she's been spotted, and when a bottle of complimentary champagne arrives at your table courtesy of the owner you understand, you tell the waiter to give him your thanks. The champagne isn't great, fairly cheap, and you can see Eloise almost grimace as she tastes it but she doesn't say anything, finishes her glass, doesn't object when you pour her another.

The whole dinner is nothing amazing, it's nothing particularly remarkable, it's characterised by the now standard number of pictures Eloise takes, you get a text asking if you're in the city so you know you've been tagged, you know you're back to being always online, but in this city you almost don't mind, you grew to loathe it before you left, and though you now view it with the kind of reverence that only comes from distance, you're still somewhat resentful, you want people to know yes you're back in town, yes you're with Eloise, yes she's amazing in every way, yes you're doing well. You know it's stupid but you don't choose to feel this way, and you want to fight it but know it's a fight you can't win, and so you ignore it, let it happen, try not to look too smug when you smile.

Eventually the meal is over, Eloise picks up the bill despite you trying to, she insists, she says *I have no idea how much money you have but without wanting to sound like a bitch it's going to be significantly less than I do, so let me, I don't mind, this money will not run out.* And though you know she should sound like a bitch saying this she doesn't, you love her and so she could say anything and you wouldn't think she sounded like a bitch. You haven't seen either of the people you know and you're disappointed but when you're standing outside, Eloise asking where to next, you feel a tap on your shoulder and turn around and there one of them is, she's smiling and says hi and you say hi back and exchange a brief hug. You're aware of Eloise's presence, but she doesn't react, you're glad because you don't know her well enough to know how she'd react in this situation, she doesn't seem at all bothered. You introduce the pair, *Eloise this is my friend from way back, friend this is Eloise, my girlfriend*, and your friend *says I know who she is, Eloise Dunhill of course*, and then playfully *What's she doing with you?* And you laugh and say *Search me!* And there's polite laughter all round. Your friend is apologising, saying *I saw you come in but you can see how busy it is, this is the first chance I've had to slip away, I didn't even know you were in the city* and you say *It's spontaneous, it's a last-minute thing, I would have texted or called otherwise* and she says it's OK, she doesn't live the freedom-filled life anymore but she can remember; her having a child means everything is meticulously planned, and you can't imagine that but you pretend anyway, you smile and nod.

She asks what you're up to and you say you've brought Eloise to meet your mother, and this makes both the women smile, Eloise coyly, your friend in a more straightforward fashion, and then she's saying are you free Sunday and you look at Eloise and she nods and you say you have no plans, what are you thinking? And your friend says she doesn't know but has no plans, her child is at a birthday party but she isn't going, she's dropping her off and picking her up, and you say *OK, give me a call and we'll arrange something* and she says she will, listen she has to get back inside, and you say OK but before she goes there are the requisite pictures, she wants photographic proof she's met Eloise and you take the phone, snap the two of them together, and you know it's just more online fodder, you know these are snapshots of your life from yet another angle, you could argue but why bother? It won't achieve anything. She finally manages to drag herself inside and it's just you and Eloise, and her phone isn't away, she's taking pictures of the two of you, the marina is behind you now and she uses it as the backdrop, she lets it frame the pair of you, and you smile, you hold her, kiss her, do whatever she requests, but you don't look at the pictures afterwards, these pictures aren't for you, they're not even really for Eloise, they're for the world, not that you think the world will care too much but Eloise cares enough to want to show the world, and while she's uploading them you ring a taxi. It's on its way, you want to go to a club with Eloise, you want to show her it, and she nods and agrees and says she's excited, she's enjoying this, and you say just you wait.

*

You're a lot less introspective once you've fallen in love.

*

The taxi ride isn't far, maybe five minutes, but the walk would've taken half an hour and it's getting cold, the night is drawing in, though it's only eleven when you reach the club. You can't remember the last time you arrived sober, it's been years, and after a quick calculation you decide about six years, and though you've not been often in the intervening years, every time you have been you've been very drunk, it's normally the only way to handle the place, but you think now, with Eloise by your side, you'll cope just fine. The club is called Welly, you tell her, actually the Wellington Club but everyone calls it Welly, in fact the cool kids call it just W now, but you're not a cool kid, you weren't cool when you were a kid and you haven't got any cooler now you've grown up. You laugh as you tell her this but there's a certain truth, a certain sadness behind it, but you brush it aside, sadness is not the way to start a night out, and you get out of the taxi and open Eloise's door, give her your hand, and even though it's fairly early there is a queue, which you join, there's no VIP here.

You can hear people whispering about her, you hear her name said, but she either doesn't hear or has mastered blissful ignorance, and you light a cigarette and hope they don't ask for ID, in the city where you live they never do but in your home town it happens often, you're never sure why but it happens anyway. When you eventually get to the front you're OK, no problem, Eloise is asked but she has ID, you see the bouncer do a double take as he reads it, he hasn't recognised her but he feels some kind of meaning in her name, he's seen it somewhere, but he must not be able to make the connection because he hands it over without a word, and you walk in, pay the entry, and then you're inside. The entranceway is quiet, two old wooden doors you think are older than you do an incredible job of hiding the noise, it's only when you open them that it hits you, dance music blasting into your every pore. You immediately need a drink, a cigarette, and you take Eloise's hand, lead her to the bar, it's dark and already crowded and you can't risk getting separated but when you get to the bar you push her forward, it's still the same bar staff it has always been, the ones hired out of necessity not skill, the ones who only serve pretty girls and their friends, and Eloise gets served almost right away, you think the guy who serves her recognises her but you can't hear their conversation, it's too loud, you take the beer she gives to you and take her hand again, lead her away from the bar, out of the small single door leading to the only outside area.

It's crowded out here, it always is, a lot of people simply stand out here all night, it's the only place you can smoke, the only place you can have a proper conversation, and again people are pointing, hushed whispers, but Eloise is so cool it gives you confidence too, after a time you learn to ignore them, only really listening when you hear someone say what's she doing with him? And it makes you smug, and you pull her in to you and kiss her passionately, obviously, and she's overwhelmed and she says *Where did that come from?* And you just shrug. The club photographer is hovering, you didn't think they came out until later, when people were drunker, trying to catch them at their worst, and other people are asking them to take their picture but the photographer isn't interested, she's looking star-struck, and you say to Eloise *Shall we put them out of their misery?* She nods, and you turn and take the stupid plastic W they make you hold and smile, trying to look sober, being sober, though you know the photographer will be back, you won't need Eloise to capture your night this time, they'll try to catch you drunk and probably eventually succeed.

You start to tell Eloise about the place; the outside has a roof and fences weaving through it making it almost maze-like, and you tell her it used to just be this big open space, people could come and go freely, then you tell her about the period when drinks weren't allowed outside, people had picked up this great habit of throwing them over the fence and onto the road, and she says *Idiots* and you say most people in this city are. After you've each had a cigarette, Eloise has taken some pictures of you, you've noticed some people taking pictures of you under the guise of taking selfies, though from the way their cameras are angled you can tell they're hardly in their own pictures, it's mostly just Eloise, she's practically an A-lister in this one-horse city, after your cigarette butts have been discarded you take her hand and take her back inside, take her on a tour.

You head to the main room, the ballroom, you point to the stage and tell her about the gigs you've seen, tell her about the first band you came to see when you were fifteen, you'd known someone who knew someone so you'd got in early, for free, but then sat around because they wouldn't serve you, you'd watched the bands then gone home, sober, but still elated, your passion for live music ignited. You start to take her upstairs but stop before you do, pointing to the area opposite the stairs, just a square with nothing going on, but you tell her that was your area, that was where you and your friends based yourselves, where you could always be found. Then you do go upstairs, all the while Eloise is taking pictures and you think they can't be great, they'll come out dull and lifeless, uninteresting, but you realise that's beside the point, she has to take the photos no matter how they'll look, it's part of who she is.

Upstairs and you point to another stage, tell her about other, smaller bands you saw on it, tell her about how they used to have an SNES on the bar for a brief period, you'd been the king of it, having grown up with one, and you're more proud than you should be, but it's only when you see her looking proud of you that you realise how ridiculous it is, and you move on. You point to the DJ on the stage, and even though it's a Friday and he normally only does Thursdays you know the DJ, you let yourself on to the stage and he moves to stop you but then sees it's you, he smiles and hugs you and you shake hands and have a brief and silent catch-up, the words lost in the music. He slips you a couple of drinks tokens and you thank him and he says he'll text you, though you know he probably won't, it's an empty statement, and back off the stage Eloise says she wants a drink, something else, and so she goes to the bar, comes back with two beers. Then you head back downstairs, and out of nowhere she drags you into the ladies' toilet. You're not sure this is a good idea, but no one else in there seems to care, and once you're locked inside a cubicle you tell her this isn't the first time you've been in these ladies' toilets, and she looks at you then hits you, playfully, before kissing you, not so playfully. You start to get a bit wound up, more than you should in a club, and you have to stop yourselves, this isn't why you're in here, why you're in here is the little baggie of white powder you didn't know she had with her, and you each do a couple of bumps, you dust each other down, and as the feeling hits your brain you know this night will be different, this night you will show your city what you mean to be, who you've become, who you are.

The rest of the night is a blur, it's a rush of alcohol, drugs, music, moving bodies, flashes of cameras, you don't know much but you know there were too many pictures, from Eloise and the club photographers and strangers and at one point you find yourself outside, you're on Twitter and her name is coming up, she's actually trending in this city, and people keep coming up to you, and guys are hitting on her even though you're right there but you don't mind, you're confident, and she's so confident she reduces these guys to rubble, and it's hilarious. You catch a photo of yourself online and it's not as bad as you'd thought, you look inebriated but to the uninitiated eye it's impossible to tell in what way, what substance has got you to this state, and you're frequently back in the toilets, bump after bump after bump, and one visit you forget to take any drugs at all, you're kissing passionately and it all gets a bit sexual, you go too far, she gets up off her knees wiping her mouth in an unfortunately practised way and you kiss her afterwards, ignoring the taste.

In between the drinks and the drugs you're dancing, always dancing, this is the way you knew it would be, you don't see Eloise, you don't see anything, your eyes are either closed or completely out of focus, but her hand is in yours, and that's all you need. Before you know it, what seems like minutes later though you know it must be hours, the music has stopped, the lights have come up, it's too bright, you're not ready to be seen, you're not ready to stop. The bouncers usher you out, offering goodnights, goodbyes, and on the streets are throngs of people, humans in all conditions of life, and still they're approaching you, endless pictures are still being taken, you eventually stop even looking at the people shaking your hand, the drugs start to wear off and it all becomes tiresome. You ask Eloise what she wants to do and she says home, hotel, she says she's no longer high and just tired, and you say OK, you ring a taxi, but they have a wait, they all have a wait, and so you say to her the hotel isn't far away, lets walk it, and you light a cigarette with a shaking hand, you try to anyway but you're incapable, you're glad when she takes it from you and does it for you.

Cigarette in one hand, Eloise's hand in the other, you're alive to the sounds of the night. You can hear shouting, the usual drunks trying to impress, the ones who have become primal and are trying to be the dominant one in the pack, and you're glad you're not like them, you haven't met any of Eloise's male friends, does she even have any? And you hope they're not like that, it's not for you. You eventually make it back to the hotel and it's quiet, the lobby is deserted, and you're glad for this as you basically stumble into the lift, by now you've come down, you want more drugs but one look at her tells you it's not going to happen, she looks like she's asleep already, and it takes a lot of cajoling to get her to leave the lift and get into the suite. She goes straight to the bedroom and asks if you're coming and you say *Yes, just going to the toilet*, and by the time you get to bed she's gone, she's a million feet under, she's dead to the world. You try to wake her, ask her if she wants to get undressed but she's unresponsive so you do it for her, you slip off her dress and bra and put her in a tee shirt you brought, tuck her in properly and kiss her softly.

You're not high but not ready for sleep yet, so you head back into the living area of the suite, then collapse on the couch, flick through the channels but there's nothing going on, it's 4am and it's all just crap. You take your phone out of your pocket and, grimacing, decide for some reason this is the time to review the photos, all one billion of them, from the last week. You start at Facebook, the number of photos on your profile has jumped from zero into the thousands, and you know you'll never get through them all so you pick some at random, and in them all you look so happy, you carry a smile you didn't realise you were capable of making, Eloise is in most of them and she's smiling too, she looks even happier than you remember, and these ideas combine to make you smile now, here on this couch in this hotel in the middle of the night. And you begin to think it's not so bad, all of this, maybe this is what the future is, maybe you're a dinosaur for trying to avoid it all. You wonder if all along she's been right and you've been wrong, and the more you look at the pictures the more you think maybe you should just surrender.

In this moment you want to tell her you love her, you love her more than anyone ever has or ever will love anything, but standing in the door to the bedroom you see she's still out for the count, and she looks so peaceful lying there you can't bear to disturb her. Instead you undress, lie next to her, kiss her gently again and pick up your phone. You decide this is it, it's time, I give up, I'm getting an Instagram account. You only want to so you can look through her pictures, you'll probably never upload any of your own, but this is still a sacrifice on your part, you feel like a good person for coming to this resolution. You look at her, lying there, and think she'll be proud of you, and it's with this thought in your head that you drop off, sleep takes you away.

Saturday morning hits you hard, it makes you hurt. When you initially wake you have no idea where you are, and panic begins to spread through your body before you remember the hotel, the city, you slowly remember last night. But this early, your phone tells you it's not even 7am yet, it's too hard to handle, too much to comprehend, and so you roll over and go back to sleep. When you next wake it's with Eloise gently shaking you, she tells you it's eleven and she wants you to get up, she wants more of the tour. When you're able to open your eyes and look at her she looks perfect, an angel in a dream, she must have been up for a while because her hair is wet, showered probably, but she's dressed, and she looks bright and full of life. She says *I've ordered breakfast from room service, you should have enough time to shower before it comes,* so you drag yourself into it, and as you emerge she's plating a nice big breakfast, it looks like it contains all the meat and grease you'll need to get through the day.

As you eat it, slowly at first, but then with more vigour, soon you're wolfing it down, you text your mother, asking about times and plans and she says the table is booked for eight, it was a squeeze but you got a reservation, and you say you'll head to hers for around seven, you want her to meet Eloise before you're out in public, you want to explain to her beforehand, not during or after, why people are staring, and pointing, and whispering, which you're sure they will be, but you don't tell her this yet, in a text, you just say you'll see her at seven. Eloise has been photographing you while you text, and she says it's cute, how close you are to your mother, she says she's jealous because it's never been that way for her, and this makes you sad to hear so you get up and pull her to her feet, hold her, say in her ear that your mother will love her, because you're sure she will, and that she has a family, you're her family now, and you hear a sniff and when you look at her she's crying, but despite the tears rolling down her face you can tell it's because she's happy, and she can barely whisper thank you before she collapses into your arms and the two of you stand there, holding each other, loving each other.

Once the food has had time to settle, once Eloise has reapplied the make-up that ran in streams down her face, once you're dressed, you tell her the tour will resume now, you're not sure where but you propose to wing it, she says *Shall I drive?* And you say *Yes, this tour is going to take you all over the city.* When you're in the car you realise the easiest way to do this will be chronologically, and so you direct her to the street you first lived on, the house you grew up in, and though you've not been inside for almost fifteen years you've been outside it so many times, it seems much smaller now, but in most ways it looks the same, the front door has changed but the numbers are the same, the ivy your mother so carefully cultivated to grow up the front of the house, the bay windows, the attic window you can just about see from ground level, it's all the same. You tell her this is where you lived when your family was whole, before your parents split, before they went their separate ways. She looks sad but you tell her it's OK, it was for the best, it changed things but not for the worse. You point to a tree stump, you tell her it used to be a chestnut tree that went as high as you could see, when you were young you were convinced it went all the way to space, and you tell her about the conkers it used to drop, how you used to collect the biggest to take to school. You tell her about the time the cat went missing, he was gone for two weeks, and you were terrified he would never come home but he did, one day, it was your birthday, and it was the best present you could have hoped for.

After standing for a time in silence, you're reflecting, she's trying to imagine a younger you running and playing and laughing, you get back in the car and drive to the end of the street. You park again and cross the main road your old street emerges on to, and then you're in a park. It's not the biggest, it's mostly just grass with a small playground, but you tell her this is where you spent your time, as a child, this is where you and your friends came to play football, to run around and do all the stuff kids do. You sit with her on the swings and tell her about the time you came to play football, you forwent watching your favourite TV programme, *Buffy the Vampire Slayer*, because you wanted to play with your friends, and you'd set a tape to record it but you'd forgotten to rewind it, so the programme hadn't recorded, you tell her how sad you were when you got home. You can't help but smile at the simplicity of it all, and when you zone back into the real world Eloise is taking pictures of you, the park, and you wonder if these will be uploaded as per usual, or if they'll get their own album, your own album of your life, you wonder if this is her way of integrating herself into your past.

When you're back in the car you take her to your primary school, full of happy memories, then your high school, the not so happy memories, and then to your college, happy memories again. They're all next to each other, you could walk between them all in less than ten minutes, and she's enraptured as you talk about them, you tell her about your year ten English teacher who inspired you, about the time you got in trouble for laughing at the substitute maths teacher who couldn't control the class, you tell her about the friends you made, the friends you lost, all the things that happened to a younger you. Just round the corner from the college is the house your grandmother used to live in, the one she lived in for almost all of your childhood, and you take her to the field at the end of the street that used to have a school, one that's long gone now, a school that your parents wanted to send you to until you kicked and screamed loud and long enough to make them change their minds.

Then you head to the small village you lived in for a time, you drive past another old house, you don't stop because the memories are mixed, love and death and loss intertwined in ways you're not ready to explain yet. Instead you take her to the pub at the end of the street, The Cross Keys, and you tell her how you used to come most nights a week as a late teenager, you and your friend would drink beer and play pool and life was simple. You tell her about the Christmas Eves you've spent here, how it's a tradition to come, one you've skipped only once in ten years, and you promise her you'll take her this year, show her what it's all about. As you sit in the pub, a drink each, nostalgia washes over you, threatens to overcome you, but you mostly have it under control, you're glad that Eloise is taking pictures, texting, Facebooking, Instagramming, you're glad for the not too extended silences, because it allows you to think, it allows you to remember, it allows the past to come to life in a way that, for the first time in a long time, isn't haunting. You realise the past only haunted you because you were a ghost in the present, because you weren't human, but now that you are, now that Eloise has made you a real person, the past has no fear, no regret, the past is the past, the present is what's important, her.

Later in the afternoon and you're still in the pub, a few drinks down, not drunk, it's a quiet Saturday afternoon and as it's a small village pub mostly filled with old people, no one has recognised Eloise, and it seems as if she's basking in the anonymity of it all. She's been taking pictures all day, almost constantly when she hasn't been driving, and you let her, you know she won't spend much time here, after all you never do, so you know she needs to capture it. She knows it's important to you, these places helped shape who you are, made you into the person you are, the person she loves, and you know that's what she's trying to grasp, and so when she insists on your smiling and sticking out your tongue and looking serious and whatever else you indulge her, you try to make her happy. Before long it's late afternoon, the early evening is creeping in, and though it's earlier than you said you'd be at your mother's it's only ten minutes from the pub, and you decide to surprise her.

Upon arrival at her house, in the next village, an even smaller one, one that on a sunny day like today is idyllic, the garage door is open, she's been gardening, you know this even though she's nowhere to be seen. After Eloise has parked you take her hand, she's nervous, you understand, you can tell by the look on her face but more so by the fact her phone is not in her hand, it's in her bag, she's not even holding it for comfort like she often does, she's holding you instead. You lead her around the side of the house, down the narrow passage, and quickly scanning you see your mother isn't in the garden, you can see her in the conservatory. She doesn't see you, she never does when you come this way, you guess she never expects it, it's only when you reach to open the door she looks up and smiles, and her smile is filled with warmth, and she gets up as you enter and you hug, a long, deep hug, and you say hello and she kisses you and says hello you. She notices the figure lurking behind you, looking tiny and scared, and you say *Mother, this is Eloise. Eloise, this is my mother.*

There's a tentative handshake, your mother is relaxed, she always is since she retired, but Eloise is on edge, and so Eloise doesn't say anything, she stands there meekly, and you motion for her to have a seat and she does, relieved to have something to do, and your mother asks if you'd like a drink and you say yes, Eloise nods slightly and your mother goes off to get them. Normally you would, it's become your role in this house when you visit, but you don't want to leave Eloise and your mother alone just yet, and your mother must have sensed this and you love her for it. She returns with a beer for you, and a gin and tonic for Eloise, and one for herself. Eloise thanks her quietly and takes the drink, sips it, holds on to the glass as if she might disappear otherwise, and you and your mother talk, catch up. Though you talk on the phone fairly frequently it's different when you're together, you've always much more to say, and you ask about her partner, what time he's expected, you ask about the garden, what she's been up to, all the usual things.

You can see on her face that the drink is relaxing Eloise, the longer she sits in the chair without your mother eating her alive the more comfortable she becomes, and soon she starts chipping in to the conversation, when your mother asks what you've been doing with your time Eloise offers some suggestions, volunteers some information, and soon, as you knew it would be, they're getting along like old friends. Your mother asks how you met, and you tell her about the pub, how it all began, how it's been something of a whirlwind but in the best possible way, and your mother is smiling and nodding and she looks pleased. Eloise excuses herself and asks very politely where the toilet is, and when she's gone and it's just you and your mother, your mother is saying how pretty she is, how nice she seems, and you agree, telling your mother that Eloise is, quite simply, the best.

At some point your mother's cat stalks in, immediately sits in the chair that Eloise has vacated as if he owns it, and you concede, as you always do, that he has more right to it than you, or than Eloise, he lives here after all. He pretends not to know you as he always does, but it doesn't last long, it never does, and soon he's sitting on you, rubbing on you and purring, and you look up to see Eloise with her camera, snapping away, and this is when you're fully relieved, you know she's comfortable, you're so happy. The doorbell goes and you hear the familiar shout of hello! And you know it's your mother's partner, and while she goes to greet him Eloise sits back in the chair, next to you, and kisses you and you kiss her and you say *I'm proud of you, you're doing really well,* and she strokes the cat and says how nice your mother is, even despite all you'd told her she's surprised, and you're pleased, delighted in fact.

Your mother returns with her partner, he complete with a gin and tonic of course, and you greet him, shaking hands, ask him how he is and he asks you, and you introduce him to Eloise, and she offers another awkward handshake, but soon the four of you have moved to the living room, there's room enough for you all in here, and you're talking as if you've known each other forever, which of course you and your mother have. The cat follows you in and proceeds to climb all over your mother's partner, you think he does it for fun because your mother's partner isn't entirely comfortable with him, and you think the cat does it just to annoy him. But soon he gives it up and then he's sitting on Eloise, purring, and she's delighted and you're delighted and your mother is saying to her partner *You see, this is how it works, one day you'll learn.*

Another round of gin and tonics is consumed and then your mother and her partner both disappear to get changed, and the cat follows, so it's just you and Eloise, and as soon as you two are alone her phone is out, she's photographing you, the pair of you, the house, and she asks for a tour of the garden and while you're walking around she's taking photos of everything, of the pair of you in front of everything, and while she's uploading the pictures you kiss the top of her head, tell her how happy you are with how well it's going, and she says she's happy too and you tell each other you love each other, and the gushing of love and photographs is only interrupted by your mother shouting that the taxi is here, it's time to go.

The meal is a resounding success. You've prepared Eloise to be recognised and of course she is, not by the other patrons, who are blissfully unaware, but by the staff, the waiters and waitresses and the people behind the bar; the place seems to employ exclusively teenagers, they're all young and beautiful, which means in some strange, sort of hopeless way they look up to Eloise. But she smiles, she's polite. You've forgotten to tell your mother what's going on but she barely seems to notice, or if she does she ignores it, and you're grateful for this.

The food is incredible, as it always is, this is by far and away the best restaurant in the city, and you all have starters, mains, desserts, finding room in yourselves you wouldn't normally, not wanting to pass up the opportunity. You share bottles of wine, white and red and rosé, and your mother has cocktails, not enough to get drunk, enough to enjoy herself, and you and her partner have a couple of ales each, and by the time the bill comes it's like you're an old family, it's like this is just another evening in a series of evenings that have been your life. The bill sits a long time ignored, you've so much to talk about, at some point Eloise outs herself, she talks about her parents and the hotels and she says she's at art school and you tell your mother she's actually a really good artist, and Eloise says a model too and you can't help the shadow that passes over your face as she says this but no one notices, it's left unsaid, and the conversation continues to flow. At one point your mother grabs a waitress who's passing and tipsily asks her to take a picture, and she agrees, saying *Cheese!* And you all smile, you have your arm around Eloise, your other around your mother, and you almost can't believe the two most important women in your life get along so well, you can't believe how lucky you are, and so for a while you let the conversation pass over you, you just sit there content, thinking how wonderful it all is, and it's only when you're blinded by a flash you realise there are more pictures, your mother is now taking pictures of you and Eloise together, some of them are for your mother, others are for Eloise, they seem to share a common need to capture the moment, though you know this is just the drink in your mother, it's not an actual compulsion like it is for Eloise.

Soon you're outside, the evening is brisk, you didn't bring a jacket but you didn't need to, you're warm, and besides you're wrapped up in Eloise, the wine has gone to her head and she's not making any attempt to hide her affection, and though you're a little embarrassed it's only a little, really you like it, and you're reassured by the beaming grin on your mother's face, you can tell how happy she is. The taxi soon arrives and you all pile in, heading back to your mother's for a nightcap, and you've told her already about the hotel and you plan to get a taxi to it later and she understands, she has needs just like any other person and though this is not said, it's never said, it's an understanding between adults and it is known.

Back at the house Eloise is in full picture mode, you all have gin and tonics and Eloise is drunkenly chasing the cat, she wants to love him, and you try to tell her it's not going to happen, he's timid, startled by large groups and loud noises but she's not listening and so you let her, you sit with your mother and her partner and try to act less drunk than you are. They're both full of dignity, as always, and you're slurring, as usual, but they don't seem to mind, apart from slurring you're basically acting like yourself, everything is OK. Soon Eloise tires of chasing the cat and joins you in the living room, and she is rewarded when he creeps in, he ignores her and heads for your mother but Eloise is content to take pictures of him, of your mother, and you're not sure if she'd like to be on the internet but she's not of your generation, she doesn't use the internet in the way you do, she'll never know, it'll never affect her, and so you don't stop Eloise, you just let her do what she likes doing so much.

After another gin and tonic each there are yawns all round, Eloise is practically asleep on you, and you order a taxi and as it heads to the house you say your goodbyes, Eloise musters a sleepy *Thanks for having me, it's a pleasure to meet you both, I hope I see you again soon* before she finally passes out on the couch, exhausted, drunk. You're shaking your mother's partner's hand and hugging your mother, and quietly they're both saying *Hold on to her, she's great, she seems really nice*, and you're grinning like the drunk in love fool you are and saying don't you worry, she isn't going anywhere, and you all laugh quietly, drunkenly, not wanting to wake her up and there's a beep and it's the taxi. You wake Eloise up, she's reluctant but you eventually put her in the taxi, and with one more round of goodbyes the taxi pulls away, you see your mother waving from the doorstep before the door closes, she's back inside, and you prop Eloise up on yourself, instead of her lying down uncomfortably she's now leaning on you, and she must sense it because without waking she wraps her arms around you, and you hold her, appreciate her, appreciate her presence without the camera being with you.

The taxi driver is talking but you're not listening, you're tired now, and he winds his way through dark streets and you think he's going a bit fast but you don't drive, haven't for a long time, and besides you're drunk so you're in no place to criticise. You see a flash, and you brace yourself for more pictures, Eloise must be awake, but as you look at her she's still asleep, her phone is nowhere to be seen, and you hear a horn blaring and you realise the flash is coming from in front, it's not a camera flash but head-lights, they blind you as the horn deafens you and you feel the taxi lift up in the air, it's dark and you're disorientated but you know you're upside down, and there's a crashing sound, a pain unlike any you've ever felt rips through your head, and then it's just black.

3

The pain is blinding, crippling, it's all you can feel. You try to open your eyes and you succeed but only a fraction, and only for a second. You can see wires, a monitor, you can hear a faint beeping, as if it's far away, in a dream. You try to move your arms but you get no response, none from your legs either. You try to move your head and it moves the tiniest bit, but you're not strong enough to stop it from quickly falling back into its original position. You can hear someone talking, but it sounds like they're underwater. He's awake, a voice says, but then it's all black again.

The next time you wake the pain is less intense, though it's still there. This time your eyes open fully, though you can't see anything, the world is out of focus. You try to move your arms again and you do, only a little, but enough to reassure you they're not lost. You can still hear the beeps, you can vaguely hear a conversation, someone's crying, asking what's going to happen, and you want to speak, want to be involved, but all you can do is croak. But this is enough. Immediately there's a shadow, someone is looming over you, and you want to reach out and touch them but you can't, all you can do is make your arm tremble for a second before the effort overwhelms you and you have to stop. Far away, you feel someone take your hand. As they do you feel relief in your veins, you feel the pain subside, and for a second everything is OK – but then you're gone again.

This time things are clearer, your eyes open fully and it only takes a minute or two before they focus. You don't recognise your surroundings: you're in a bed, not one you know; it's small, fairly uncomfortable. You can see a window but from the angle you're lying at all you can see through it is sky, so you can't make a guess where you might be. You look down at yourself and you can see things stuck to you – stuck to your chest, there's something clipped to one of your fingers, there's a tube stuck in your right arm, in the crook of your elbow joint. There's someone at the foot of the bed – they look sad, they've been crying – and soon you realise it's your mother, and she sees you looking at her and she bounds over and kisses you, kisses the top of your head, but it hurts, it feels raw, and you try to break away, to make her stop.

She does eventually stop, and you try to talk but your throat feels like you've swallowed a razor blade, it's like you've been eating sand, and all that comes out is a coarse whispering sound, like a tiny car failing to start. Your mother asks if you want some water and you just about manage to nod, though it takes every single ounce of effort you possess. She puts a straw in your mouth and you're able to suck, pulling the water into your mouth, feeling an almost instantaneous relief as it floods your mouth, rehydrates you, but it's too much and you begin to cough, then you vomit, and you're embarrassed and confused and you try to wipe your mouth but it's too much effort to move your arms that far and you start to cry, and you're glad when your mother picks up a tissue and cleans you up. You try to talk again and it's more than before, though still too hard for you. You manage a dry, rasping, *Where?* And then you stop, the effort is too much, and you look at your mother in what you hope is an enquiring fashion and she bursts into fresh tears. The sight breaks your heart and confuses you even more; you want to take her hand but you can't, and so you lie there.

Soon another woman enters, she looks like a nurse but you can't be sure, and when she sees you're awake she calls for a doctor and soon a man bustles into the room. He begins to prod and probe you. He shines a light in your eyes – it's so bright, and for a second you almost remember something, something important, but as soon as it almost comes it's gone, and you're back in the room. He's asking questions but you can't understand them; all you can do is look at the people swarming around you – but it's so much effort, you're so tired, and it's not long before there's black again.

When you next see the world, it's all beginning to make sense. This time you're woken by an external force: there's another nurse bustling around you, she's lifting you up and changing your pillows, she's reading things on a chart and writing things, and when she sees you're awake she says, *Hello, how do you feel?* And again you can't talk, but after some water – only a little, you do not want to be sick again – you're able to respond. You tell her you're tired, you hurt, you're confused. You ask her where you are and she says the hospital, and this makes sense, the room you're in confirming her statement. She asks if you would like to see your mother, she's just gone to get a coffee, and you nod, manage a faint please, and then she's gone.

The nurse returns soon after with your mother and the doctor you saw previously, and they're talking to each other as they enter, but this stops when they both see you're awake. Your mother starts to cry again but the doctor looks pleased. He says, *Good morning, how do you feel?* You repeat your earlier statement – tiredness, pain, confusion – and he tells you it's understandable, it's likely to be this way for some time, he's just glad you're awake, they all are. You ask him what happened, how you got here, and as you say this he looks at your mother, she looks at him, and something passes between them – a shadow, a ghost – and suddenly you're afraid, more scared than you've ever been. The fear takes over and before you black out you can only whisper *Eloise*…

This time you're woken by the feel of water. In your dream you're swimming but in reality it feels warm. You're not in the ocean, and when you realise you've wet yourself you begin to cry – the confusion takes over and crying is all you can muster. This time it's your father in the room; you recognise him immediately even through your tear-blurred eyes, and he gets up from the solitary chair, still at the foot of your bed, like a vigil, and this word scares you, it can't be. Your father stands beside you and takes your hand, he dabs at your tears with a tissue, and soon a nurse enters, a different one, and she's taking your gown off, washing you, putting a fresh gown on, and you want to thank her but you're ashamed and so you just keep crying, feeling useless, confusion all you know.

When you're eventually able to get yourself under control, you ask for more water and drink it slowly again, not tempting fate, sick of vomiting, and this time when you try to talk the words come out stronger than they have done previously, you can hear your voice and you sound like yourself, and for a second this comforts you, but only for a second. You ask your father where you are and he repeats what the nurse told you previously. He says you're in the hospital, and you ask which one and he says the one in your home city, in his city, and you ask why you're there and he falters – he doesn't know what to say. But looking up at the lights in the room, above you, shining on you, you remember. A light brighter than any you've ever seen, the noise, being thrown around like a toy, the pain, and it's all come flooding back to you.

Your father goes and is replaced by your mother. You want to ask her what happened, but you don't care; you want to ask if you're OK, what injuries you have, but they don't matter. All you want to know is whether Eloise is OK, and you ask your mother and she immediately bursts into tears and this tells you it all, this is more honest than words could ever be, and you feel your entire life drop out from under you.

You ask again, you beg your mother not to say it, but you already know she can't not. You already know what's coming, and you can feel the wind rushing in your ears, you see stars in front of your eyes, you can hear a million voices in your head all shouting different things, screaming at you not to listen, screaming at you not to ask, screaming at you not to find out. But you have to – it's all you are right now – and you ask your mother what happened to Eloise and she says, *I'm so sorry, Eloise didn't make it.* You knew these words were coming but you don't understand it, you mistake their meaning. You say, *That's OK, she can't be here all the time, when is she coming?* And your mother, still crying, says, *No, you don't understand – I'm so sorry, Eloise is dead.*

The pain is back, but it's a different pain, you can't even feel your body anymore, you're not sure if it's the drugs or the healing or what, but your body doesn't belong to you anymore, nothing does. People are in the room, talking to you, their voices are saying things that you know you'll never hear, and even if you did hear them you'd never understand. She's dead, that's all you know. That's all there is that exists anymore. People are trying to get your attention. They want answers, they want to know about you, inside you where they can't see, they don't know, but you're not there, you're in another world, you're in a different universe where this bed, this room, this hospital, these things don't exist – all that exists is you and her. And you can feel the tears on your cheeks but you're not crying – you can't anymore, there are no more tears. You're empty. You're empty in every possible way.

Food is placed in front of you, and various drinks, but they don't mean anything, you wouldn't know what to do with them even if you wanted to try, you can't move, your body is unresponsive. Someone touches your head, you don't know who, and far away you feel a jolt, something sharp, but it's a million miles away, it's not relevant. You just want these people to go away, you want them to be replaced by her, but you know this can never be, you know this is how it's going to be, but you don't accept this, you can't, and people drift in and out of the room, in and out of your consciousness but they don't matter, nothing matters. Soon it's all black, you must be asleep, but even if you're dead you don't care, you don't think you're capable of caring anymore.

Someone is saying please, please God please just answer, and you can see your mother, but she's on the other side of a veil, she lives in a different world to you now, and she's saying please just answer, say anything, and you want to respond, if only to tell her to leave, but you can't, she's so upset but you can't do anything about it, you can't do anything about anything. You're underneath the veil now, and you can never emerge from it, you'll have to wear it for the rest of your life, for as long as you live and she doesn't, it's your new shadow, it's the new you.

A drink is put in front of you, a straw is put in your mouth, but it just lolls there, you don't have the energy to drink from it. You don't even know if you're thirsty, you can't tell, you can't feel, someone is saying you haven't drunk anything for so long, please don't make them use a drip, but even as you hear these words you know they're going to have to, you know you're not capable of taking the liquid on board, and later you can see someone attaching something to your arm, it must be the drip someone mentioned earlier, and people are crying, but when you move your hand to touch your face you're not one of them, your face is bone dry, in fact all you can feel on your face is bones, a skeleton's head, one that once belonged to you, belonged to her, but now doesn't belong to anyone. Your head drops to the side, you can't even hold it straight anymore, and you sleep.

Time passes by, you know this because the sky outside the window goes dark and then light and then dark again, over and over again. You don't know how much time has passed, how long you've been in this bed, how long since...

The accident, you're finally able to bring yourself to think, but you don't care how long it's been. All you want to do is see her, tell her you love her, tell her you'll make everything OK, and when you realise this will never happen you can't even cry, the hole inside you is so big that nothing can emerge from it, not even tears.

The only thing that eventually brings you slightly back into the world is when someone who looks like your mother, it might be her but you don't know, you don't recognise anyone, anything, when the woman says the word funeral. This pulls you back to reality, you're able to look at her and whisper *When?* and she asks you what you said but you don't repeat yourself, you just look at her, and she must realise what you said because she says she doesn't know when, they're holding the body for an autopsy, her parents aren't happy about the delay, it's pretty clear cut but until the case is over she can't be buried, and at this word you do cry. Buried, the one you love the most in the world being put into a hole in the ground, you can't accept this, and you want to stop it, you sit up, you must see her, have her, but when you try to get out of bed hands are holding you back, pushing you down, and you don't have any strength, you immediately fall back, and your mother takes your hand and tells you she loves you and tells you she's sorry, but the words don't mean anything, not anymore.

You finally eat something, you nibble some toast. You don't know where it came from but you're almost grateful for it. Hunger is the first thing you've felt in so long, and feeling hurts, not this specific feeling but just feeling at all, and so you eat to be rid of it, but before long you feel sick, a few bites is too much, and you lie back, groaning. Your mother is still there and you ask how long it's been and she says a month, she says it in a way that makes you think that the news should surprise you but it doesn't, it barely even registers. You ask her what happened and she looks away, she doesn't want to answer, but when you press her she does, eventually.

She says you were in a taxi, she and her partner had gone to bed and you and, she hesitates before saying her name, you and Eloise had got into a taxi back to the hotel, but because you were drunk and she was asleep neither of you noticed the taxi driver was drunk too, he was driving erratically, too fast, he was using his phone, texting while he was driving, and he lost control around a corner and hit another car head on. She stops, but you push her, you want to know, and she says Eloise died instantly, and you know you're supposed to feel relieved, you know you're supposed to concentrate on the word instantly, but all you hear is the word died. It's all you know.

She says the driver was injured but not seriously, his seatbelt and airbag saved his life. You ask about the other car and your mother says it was a family, two parents and a young child, all dead, and you can't believe it. Why you, why did these four people have to die, why not the driver, what spared the two of you? You ask your mother but without hope of an answer, she doesn't know, she can't know, and now you do cry, but you don't cry because of Eloise, or the young family, you don't cry because they're dead, you cry because you're alive.

A fractured skull, a sprained wrist, multiple broken ribs, a punctured lung and a broken leg. When you're finally able to ask, this is what you are told the damage you sustained was. The doctor said it was touch and go for a while, you were in a coma for three weeks, but you're not really listening, you're wishing it had been less touch and more go, you don't know where you would have gone but you know Eloise would have been there, and that's the only place you want to be, no matter where in existence it is.

Eventually you're allowed home, not to your own home, you're taken to your mother's, she's going to look after you until you're fully better. When the doctor says this your mother looks at you, and you look at her, but your face is saying but that's never going to happen, I'm never going to be fully better, but the doctor doesn't hear this, or if he does he chooses to ignore it, and he continues to go through the housekeeping of your release.

You spend your days in bed, looking at but not seeing the TV, hearing but not listening to music, the radio, and at various points there is a cat on you but when there is all you're able to do is hold him and cry, and it's never long before he squirms out of your grasp, runs away, and you're alone again.

There's a trial, but you're not present, not really. You're called as a witness but nothing you're able to say helps, you tell them you can't remember, your head has been opened since, and nothing remains inside it. Your mother testifies on your behalf, she talks about you being drunk, Eloise being drunk and asleep, she starts crying and says she almost lost you, and pointing at the driver, who has bags under his eyes, he's looking down, he looks empty, your mother points at him and says it's his fault, he killed four people, and she apologises to some people who might be relatives of the family also killed but you don't ask, all you want to do is go home. You can feel the driver looking at you, meekly, but you can't look at him, you know you should look at him, look him in the eyes, you know you should hate him, feel nothing but burning rage for all he is and all he's done, all he's taken from you, but you can't. All you can do is wait for it to be over, and after what seems like a lifetime, though Eloise isn't around so you know it's only this lifetime, it'll always only be this lifetime, you hear the word guilty, and when you're home you hear your mother say life, no possibility of release, and she says this in a way that you know is meant to comfort you but it doesn't, you don't feel a thing.

4

You'd wanted to tell Eloise everything, to have her know everything about you. All the depression, all the heartbreak, the suicide attempts, the months without feeling, the way you'd completely and utterly given up. The love of your life who'd broken up with you, the girl who'd fucked your best friend, the girl who'd been everything, then told you she'd be happier if you died.

You'd wanted to tell Eloise that she'd saved you from all that, but you didn't get the chance, and now you never would. You'd never be able to explain your past, how it affected your present, but how it would no longer define your future. Not since she came along. The girls you'd loved and lost, the voids you'd fallen into – everything in your past that you thought was killing you, but was actually leading you to her. Every terrible thing that had happened to you, that had been totally worth it.

5

Eventually you're allowed to go home, properly go home, your mother drives you back to Leeds, neither of you saying anything as the ground passes beneath you, she's given up trying to talk to you, she knows you'll talk when you're ready. She doesn't want you to go back to Leeds, but she knows you have to; she's afraid of what you might do, but also knows she's powerless to stop it. She can't make you any better, but if she forces her will on you she can make you a lot worse, and so she takes you home. You're glad to be home, in your flat, alone, you love your mother very much but she had started to drive you mad, following you around the house, trying to make sure you're OK, asking if you're OK, if you need anything, here let me get that for you, no sit I'll do that, you take it easy. None of this was helping and she knew it, she knows exactly what you're going through, but she can't help herself, she loves you.

Once she's gone and you're locked in, alone with only your thoughts, you just stand, stand in the middle of your flat and just stare, not looking at anything, just staring. There's no food in the fridge but it's OK, you're not hungry, hunger isn't something you feel anymore. The view is still as incredible as it has always been, but it no longer moves you. Instead of looking out across the city and imagining all the people, their lives and loves and everything about them, now it taunts you, it's a spread of all the people going about their lives, living day to day, and their lives are tragedy free, they can never know your pain.

You sit on the couch, well not so much sit as drop, you're careless these days, you've nothing to care for, and you reach for the remote and turn the TV on to a random channel but you don't watch what's on, you only put the TV on because it feels like something you're expected to do. Your phone vibrates, it's been going almost constantly for weeks, months, maybe even years, you've lost all track of time, there's no point measuring it, none of it means anything to you. You've ignored it constantly all the time, you have nothing to say to anyone. A few times when you were at your mother's house she picked it up, talked into it, talked to your friends, boss, whoever, but you didn't pay any attention, you had no attention to pay, you knew she'd be saying the same stuff, about you, how you are, everything, and even though it was about you it didn't concern you, you just let her.

Now in the flat it's like a drill boring into your skull, and so you turn it off, you're sick of hearing it, the thing could vibrate every second between now and eternity but it'll never be her, it'll never be worth picking up. After sitting for a time you stand, for no particular reason, just because, you walk around, you pick things up but you don't look at them before putting them back, you don't feel them, none of this is real, nothing is anymore. You go down to the lobby and get your post, there's a huge pile of it, but you have no intention of reading any of it, and sure enough it just sits on the table unopened, unwanted, its mere presence serves only to remind you of the world you now live in and you wish you'd left it, but it's too late, you've acknowledged its presence, you can't be rid of it. It's the little things like this that move you the most, that pain you, you can see all the beauty and horror of the world and none of it even garners your attention, but something as simple as a pile of post on the table destroys you, it rips you in shreds and laughs at the pieces.

In order not to cry, or at least not to weep, you sit back on the couch, you stare at the TV, you try with everything you have to concentrate on it. It's late in the evening, your mother wanted to drop you off as late as possible in the hope you'd just fall into bed and sleep, even though she knew as well as you do that isn't going to happen but she tried anyway. It's late and you do want to get into bed but you can't, the last time you slept in that bed Eloise did too, you know it'll smell of her, and you're not ready for that yet. Aside from the trial, the funeral, you've had no reminders of her, and though you don't want to do her a disservice, you don't want to discard her memory, you're not ready to embrace it yet, you just can't. So instead you sit on the couch, you stare at the TV, and it's only when an article on the news about social media starts that you actually pay attention. It's a nonsense segment, merely a bit of name-dropping of popular tools to draw in an audience, but it moves you nonetheless. Facebook, Twitter, Instagram, Tumblr, these were her things, she owned them, you always skirted around the periphery but she was right there in the middle, making the most of all their glory, and the longer this article goes on the more it hurts, but the less you're able to drag yourself away, and soon you're lying in the foetal position, rocking back and forth, tears streaming down your face, and it's only long after the article has ended you're able to stop crying, sit back up, come back to a level almost resembling calm.

The segment moved you, but not in a way you wanted, not in a way you'd hoped, the reminders only serving to make you feel worse, and it's late but you're not tired, you know you won't sleep, you've hardly slept at all since it happened, and when you have you've been awakened by intense nightmares, so real it's as if they're happening, and it's only remembering that the worst nightmare is the one you go through when you're awake that allows you to stop panting, stop sweating, lie back down and stare at the ceiling again. You know you won't sleep so you drag yourself out of the flat, into the lift, you can't remember when your feet got this heavy, even though you can suspect, you drag yourself to the shop in your building, and you've never been more glad for self-service counters as you scan through far too much alcohol, and as you carry it back to your flat, unload it into the fridge, take the bottle of vodka to the couch without even so much as a glass, you know this isn't the answer, you know it'll only make things worse. This has always been your cure, and though nothing has ever been this bad, you don't know what else to do. This has worked (it has never worked) in the past, so it might work now. The pain is on a level it has never reached before, will never reach again, a level you never thought possible, the darkness has never been this dark, the depths have never been this deep, and so you turn to the one thing you think might help. Though you know it won't. As you take the first swig from the bottle, the liquid burning every part of your body, you think to yourself this is how it is now, this is what your life is, this is how things go, so you might as well black out while they do.

When you wake up you have no idea what day it is, you don't care, the days have no meaning, no matter what day it is it'll all be the same anyway so why bother checking? You find your phone next to your bed, it's on now, you must have turned it on last night, though you don't remember doing so. You unlock it and it immediately opens up her Facebook page, you're on her news feed, there are messages of condolence all over it, and some of them look familiar, you must have been reading them last night, but you leave the page, close the browser, you can't face this now. You stumble out of bed just long enough to locate a half-empty bottle of rum, and taking a swig you get back into bed, today is a write-off before it's even begun.

Back in bed you pull the covers over your head so it's just you, your phone, the rum, this is all you'll need for the day anyway, and even though you don't want to you unlock your phone again, there are messages you received last night now coming through, your mother asking if you're OK, texts and WhatsApps from friends asking how you are, if they can do anything. You reply only to your mother, simply saying yes, and even though it's not true, and she'll know it, you know the only way to preserve your isolation is to text her every now and then, to keep her worries at bay, to stop her from driving and coming into your flat.

You can't stop yourself from going online, you go on Twitter, and the number of followers you have has increased again, it's been steadily increasing ever since you first met her, but they're nobody, they're hanging on to you, to her, to your relationship, they want to vicariously live through you, and you know they'll never understand that that can never happen, if you're not able to live through this how will they? There are tweets at you, direct messages, but you ignore them all, you don't care what they have to say, you have no desire to find out, you have no desire at all, except to keep drinking from the bottle you're cradling, and once it's empty to find another, and drink from that, and just keep drinking and drinking until you black out again, and then you'll start again, the sequence will repeat itself.

You only leave the bed to empty your bladder, to vomit, when violent diarrhoea strikes, but these are trips out of necessity, if you didn't have to make them you wouldn't get up at all. Without knowing it you're back on Facebook, you're back on her profile, you're looking through pictures, just pictures of her, you can't bring yourself to look at pictures of the two of you, it's too painful, you're not ready yet, and so you look at all the pictures of her, then again, a third time, until you've drunk so much you can't see them anymore, you can't focus, and it's only then you notice the smell. It's coming from the bed, it's ingrained in the sheets, it's the smell of her, and you breathe it in gratefully at first, but your gratitude doesn't last long, it turns to sadness first, then anger. Why do you have to smell this on your sheets? Why do these fucking sheets have to smell like her? Why must you be reminded of all you've lost? You get up and rip the sheets off your bed, the duvet cover and the pillowcases, and you drag them out of your apartment, you go to the rubbish room and dump them in a bin, you're in just your underwear but you don't care who sees you, that's their problem, not yours, and soon you're back in your bed, sitting on a bare mattress, and the anger has been replaced by sadness again, the anger was never really real, you weren't angry at the sheets for how they smelled, you're sad that this is the only way to smell her, you'll never smell her skin or her hair again.

Time passes, you don't know how much, you only know it's passing due to the changing colour of the sky, if not for the sky you wouldn't know time was passing at all, you'd swear you were frozen in this moment, stuck in your eternal hell. You just keep drinking, and soon you're in the bathroom, you're kneeling in front of the toilet and vomiting, first it's black liquid, all the alcohol you've drunk, then it's bile, it burns your throat and hurts your stomach, and then nothing, nothing solid comes out, you haven't eaten in… you don't know how many days, you don't keep track of time anymore, all you know is you haven't eaten in a long time, and eventually you stop retching and you lie down, you hug your knees and in the foetal position you weep, tears pool on the floor about your face and you just lie in them, unmoving, silently weeping.

Another day, maybe, or just some time later in your existence, and you're sitting at the table on your laptop, the browser is open, you have God knows how many tabs open, each of them is on a different picture of her. She's smiling, she's pouting, she looks happy and sad and angry and confused and amused all at the same time, you've tried to find her entire emotional range, you're trying to recreate her. It's not working. The drink next to you doesn't help, but you drink it anyway, you started off with a bottle of vodka but the longer you sit here, the more pictures you look at, the more your habit resembles something someone less damaged might do, after a time you got a glass, and then later some ice, and even though the drink is still straight alcohol it's less barbaric, less offensive. It's almost as if these pictures are bringing you back to life, you know they can't bring her back but you they might be able to. You've still not looked at any pictures of the two of you, that's still too hard to even think about, let alone imagine doing.

And so you click between tabs, open is Facebook, Twitter, Tumblr, you never did get around to opening that Instagram account but you may have to soon, one day you may need to unlock the secrets held within her page. But for now you just sit, and look, and cry, and drink, these are the only things you can do anymore. It's morning, you know that much, you've not particularly checked but the clock in the corner of your laptop is always there, you can't help but glance, and an hour passes, two, more hours and more drinks and more pictures and as you get drunker you feel stronger, more connected to the world, even though you know this is a temporary feeling, soon you'll pass out then wake up and you'll be gone again, but you think if you can just repeat this cycle, if you can keep this behaviour up, maybe one day you will exist in this world again.

Your phone vibrates and for once you actually look, you don't ignore it, and it's a text from your friend and it still goes unread, unanswered, but you know this is some sort of progress, you don't just turn the phone upside down or turn it off or bury it somewhere, and you're making steps. They're tiny, drunken baby steps, but steps nonetheless. And you keep looking at pictures, you're remembering her, and you keep drinking and soon it's all blackness, emptiness, you're gone.

You're in bed, you don't know how you got there, you're fully dressed and you can smell vodka, you peer down and there's an upturned bottle next to the bed, in a pool of what you must assume is the vodka you can smell, and you take off your tee shirt and throw it in the puddle, it's the best effort you can make towards cleaning it up, and instead of doing a proper job you stumble to the fridge, but it's empty, you've drunk all your alcohol. And so you grab another tee shirt, you don't know if it's clean, don't care, you simply put it on and go to the shop downstairs.

In the world you can hear hushed whispers, you can see people pointing at you, trying to be subtle and failing, and you start to cry softly, tears slowly roll down your face and your shoulders silently heave themselves up and down, it reminds you of her, you didn't mind being talked about and pointed at when you had her on your arm, she made it all worth it, she made it all OK, but now it's just you, and people know it's just you, her death made it into the papers, and now people are pointing and staring at you and you don't look at them, you just silently cry as you purchase more alcohol, you don't even look at the bottles, just take as much vodka as you can carry and go back upstairs, sit back at the table, open your laptop.

The pictures of her are all you have, you can't remember, can't access the memories you made with her, you're drunk too often, since the accident your mind has been soft, and the alcohol only makes it softer. You look at pictures of her, only her, her face and her neck and her arms and her entire body, you look and you cry, you cry for what might have been, you cry for what was. You want to call someone, to speak to someone, to hear a voice, but you don't because it won't be her, she won't answer the phone, she won't tell you she loves you, she never will again, she can't love you, she's gone, she is no more. And this makes you drink more, and cry more, and soon you're soaked in your own tears, they're dripping off you in waves but you don't, can't, dry them, all you can do is keep drinking, blink away the tears as best you can so you can see the pictures, see the photos, see her.

Soon you're off her Facebook page, you're on your own, but you're not looking at the pictures, you're not ready, instead you're looking at the tags, the check-ins, you're looking at the places you went, with her. You think back, remember meals, drinks, champagne, you remember drugs and clubs and music and movement, you remember her body against yours, the way it felt, the way it made you feel to touch her, to caress her, to love her, and you can't take it anymore, you close the laptop, you pour the glass of vodka down the sink, but it's not a reprieve, it's simply so you can just take the bottle with you to bed, and once again you're hugging it, in the bed, which still has no sheets, which probably never will again, and you drink, and drink, and drink, and then you're gone.

Today you're going to do it. You're out of bed at what seems like a reasonable time, though you're so messed up you're not sure what a reasonable time is anymore. You're sitting at your laptop. There's a drink next to you, but you're back to glasses, you have ice, you have mixer; you've made this little progress. With a shaking hand you bring the glass up to your lips and take a sip, only a small one, you're shaking too much to stand up, to refill the drink should you need to, and you're going to need the alcohol for what comes now. You open the browser, you go to Facebook, but not hers, yours. You glide past the check-ins, the tags, and you click photos. You close your eyes, sip your drink slowly, unsteadily, you tell yourself you have to do this.

Slowly you open one, then the other eye, you click the first thumbnail, and it enlarges. This is the last picture of the two of you, it's a selfie taken by her, in your mother's living room, on that night. It hurts to look at but you force yourself to, you sip the vodka for reassurance, for a material connection to the world, and you look at the picture. You're both drunk, both smiling, your arms are around her and one of hers is around you, the other disappearing into the foreground, behind the phone she's holding. She looks just like you remember her, she's small, slight, graceful, beautiful, and you break down, you can't take anymore, your silent sobs becoming a loud weeping, you pick up the glass and throw it against the wall, but when it smashes it doesn't reveal anything, the glass fragments form a pattern but it's not one you can understand, the destruction doesn't help in any way, and you drag yourself to your feet, you force your shaking legs to carry you to the fridge and you take the bottle out, then drink deeply from it, the vodka not even burning you anymore, you're so used to it, numb to it, and you don't even make it to your bed this time, you just sit in the kitchen and drink until you slump sideways, done.

You try again. The scene is the same; you're at your laptop, drink in hand, Facebook in front of you. You open the same thumbnail, the same pain floods through you, but it's less intense than before, than yesterday, or maybe earlier, you're not sure when it was you last tried. You're able to click the arrow that brings up the next photo, another of you and her. This time you both look serious, she's pouting and frowning, you've made a vain attempt at a pout but you look ridiculous, you look like you're mocking her even though you weren't, you never did. You're so engrossed in the picture that this time you don't even notice you're crying, you don't notice the tears until they're landing in your drink, you're drinking them, you don't care.

You click the arrow again and it brings another photo of you two, this time she's smiling at the camera but you're not looking at it, you're looking at her, you're lost inside her, she's smiling but you only look in love, nothing more, nothing less. This photo causes an immeasurable amount of pain and takes you from the glass, to the bottle, to your bed. This is enough for today, and so you drink.

This time you get through more photos, in them you're both laughing, you're both serious, you're both pulling goofy faces, you both look angry and confused and sad and high and drunk and clever and stupid and everything else. You knew she had the phone out always, she was always taking pictures, but you didn't realise that she had captured everything, every single facet of your short time together. You're able to get through a lot of photos, the two of you are at your mother's house, you're in the restaurant you went to that night, you're in various cities, in various clubs, other people appear in the photos but you disregard them, they're not really there, they don't know what you two know, they don't share your secrets.

Your drink sits untouched, the glass is full, but you're ignoring it. You know you're going to need it soon but you don't now, not yet, right now you're drinking her, you're drinking the pair of you, and it tastes good, it almost feels good. You only think it almost feels good because you're still not sure if you're feeling anything, right now it's just you and the pictures, you're still not in the world but that's OK, the pictures are with you, wherever you are. This place may not be existence as other people know it, but right now it's OK for you, you have what little of her you could have, and it'll do.

But soon you see yourself picking up the drink, soon you're taking it to bed, you bring the bottle, but you decant before you drink, you pour into the glass then into your mouth, and the glass, the middleman, it tells you something, but you're too drunk to know what it means, and then you're out.

6

The days begin to pass with a certain regularity, things fall into place that had not been present before. Life will never be the same, you know that, you no longer have a job, but that doesn't matter. You no longer have friends; they all moved on, got tired of you ignoring them. And though you're sad and you miss them, you don't blame them – friendship is a two-way system and you weren't present for weeks, months. You didn't try. Women come on to you, you spend a lot of time out, drinking; not as heavily as you have previously, but enough, enough to make the evenings seem less lonely, to make the nights less cold, to make yourself feel more alive. Women talk to you, they know who you are, you're semi-famous by now, but you're not interested, you can't be, it would be a betrayal, and so you politely decline, before ordering another drink.

Then one day, something amazing happens: you're not drinking. You begin to feel things, things you haven't felt for a long time. You feel hungry, you feel tired, you feel sad. It's no longer the emptiness, but it's real, physical sadness. You're so sad it physically hurts, but you welcome the pain, you know you need it. And you know why it's come about; it's all thanks to her. Every day you sit at the table, you look at your laptop, you browse through pictures of the two of you, the pictures she took. There are hundreds of them, thousands, and it takes hours of your time but every day you do it. It's become your ritual; it's become all you know. You can't have her anymore, she's gone, she's lost to you physically, but she'll never be lost to you emotionally, no one can ever take away the memories, the feelings, the photos.

You look at them every day, almost all day, and time continues to pass but now you track it, you know what day it is, what time it is. You belong to the world again. Deep down you knew you had to begin to grieve sometime, you knew there had to be a catalyst that would bring you back to life, but you didn't think, you never knew it would be this. You never even imagined that these pictures, the constant documentation of your life would be the thing that would bring you back around. It was one phone that took from you everything you had, everything you ever wanted, but it was because of another that it's all been brought back. You're amazed, and you look up, even though you don't believe in heaven, you don't believe in God or hell or anything, but you can't stop yourself from looking up and whispering *Thank you.*

7

You sit at your desk. You start your laptop. You open your browser. You load Facebook. And you begin to type.

I am so sorry, but I must join you now. I have tried and I have tried, but I have failed. You cannot join me and so I must join you. They will mourn for me, but I died a long time ago. I love you and I do this to be with you. They will miss me, but never as much as I have missed you. I'm coming.

8

8

Boyfriend of Deceased Heiress Found Dead In Apparent Suicide.

It's been less than a year since millionaire heiress Eloise Dunhill was tragically killed in a car accident, and now her former partner has been found dead in his home. Police declined to provide too many details; however they did say it looked to be a suicide, and they were not pursuing any other leads. A police spokesman said, 'Upon entering the deceased's residence we found a body in the bathroom, in the bathtub. We also found a note, of which details we will not be giving. The deceased's family has been informed.'

Patrons

Eli Allison
Rihards Ancans
Chris Barnett
Chris Bolton
Alex Boulby
Jennie Brant
Jenny Brocklebank
Tim Bugby
Martin Coates
Helen Crimmens
Mike Davidge
Terry Dean
Richard Duchemin
Paul Dunlop
Mary Elizabeth
Myles Fenlon
Georgina Florentine
Mark Gaskell
Jean Granger
Carly Granger
Emma Harper
Jeff Harris
Elliot Isaacson
Ian James
Simon Jenkins
Rachael Jones
Victor Kang
John Kelly
Steve Kerrison
Sam Knell
Epo Li
Gavin Lynch

Ian Marsden
Mike Mike
Sarah Mings
John Murphy
Niall Noonan
Yuk Mei Pang
CoF REDACTED
Edward Repton
Mike Robinson
Alex Smith
Ella Squelch
Tom Stevens
Jack Styles
Patrick Swaddle
Tim Tarry
Kuldeep Thethy
Troy Verdeer
Mike Vermourth
Becky Weale